Walk Through the Valley

Other Books by Debbie Viguié

The Psalm 23 Mysteries

The Lord is My Shepherd
I Shall Not Want
Lie Down in Green Pastures
Beside Still Waters
Restoreth My Soul
In the Paths of Righteousness
For His Name's Sake

The Kiss Trilogy

Kiss of Night
Kiss of Death
Kiss of Revenge

Sweet Seasons

The Summer of Cotton Candy
The Fall of Candy Corn
The Winter of Candy Canes
The Spring of Candy Apples

Witch Hunt

The Thirteenth Sacrifice
The Last Grave
Circle of Blood

Walk Through the Valley

Psalm 23 Mysteries

By Debbie Viguié

Published by Big Pink Bow

Walk Through the Valley

Dedicated to the fans who have loved and supported this series. Thank you all.

Thank you to everyone who helped make this book a reality, particularly Barbara Reynolds, Rick Reynolds and Calliope Collacott.

1

Church secretary Cindy Preston couldn't help but reflect that the most life-altering things in her existence happened on Sundays. It was Sunday now and as she stared into rabbi Jeremiah Silverman's eyes she knew that this Sunday was going to shake her more deeply than anything else since the death of her sister so many years ago.

They had known each other for almost two years now, and she had long suspected that he was keeping something about his past secret from her. The truth was, it was all of his past. She knew virtually nothing about his life before the day they had met over a dead body except for the fact that he had grown up in Israel. They were from two completely different worlds but every murder had brought them closer together.

And now he was looking at her with eyes that burned with an intensity that took her breath away. He had just told her that his name wasn't even Jeremiah Silverman.

She could tell he was waiting, expecting her to say something, but she in turn was waiting for him to say something more. Like why the Israeli equivalent of the CIA had given him a false name. So they stood, locked in a silence that seemed to go on forever. One of them was going to have to break it, and she realized it wasn't going to be him.

"The Mossad gave you the name Jeremiah Silverman?"

He nodded.

"And you can't tell me your real name?"

"That is also correct," he said, clearing his throat a little. His accent, which was usually very faint, had grown incredibly thick over the course of the brief conversation. It made him sound so alien to her, like someone she didn't know.

But I don't know him, she reminded herself.

"Why? Are they protecting you? Did you witness a crime or something like that?"

He shook his head. "I'm not in some kind of witness relocation program."

"Then what is it? Are you...are you a spy?" she asked, her breath catching in her throat.

He hesitated and then said very softly, "Not anymore."

She turned abruptly and sat down at the table, feeling weak in the knees. She'd known he was hiding something dark about his past. The first killer they had ever faced down together Jeremiah had shot. He had drawn a gun in the blink of an eye and only Cindy had seen it happen.

"So, you were a spy?"

He pulled out a chair and sat down gingerly, as though afraid if he got too close to her she would bolt like a skittish animal. "Intelligence gathering is just a small part of the job and it doesn't..." he stopped and looked closely at her. He sighed. "Yes, I was a spy."

Deep down she realized a tiny part of her was relieved. She had often wondered with his secretiveness and his peculiar skills if he had been a criminal of some sort. "Tell me everything."

He looked away. "I can't tell you everything. I shouldn't even have told you that much. I'm bound by an oath of secrecy and I can't break that."

2

"But you already have," she pointed out.

"You had to know that some of the attacks on Geanie were actually trying to target you and because of me."

"You said someone was trying to hurt me because they thought we were a couple," she said, feeling herself blush as she said the last word.

He nodded.

"Are they going to keep trying to kill me?"

He hesitated and her mind went into overdrive. What was it he didn't want to tell her? Was she in mortal danger even now? Or had he somehow already killed the man who had been trying to kill her? This all felt so insane.

"I do not know if you are still in danger, but I will do everything in my power to keep you safe."

"You've been thinking about leaving," she burst out, not knowing where the sudden flash of insight came from.

"I have been thinking about it for quite a while," he admitted, looking intensely uncomfortable. "I kept telling myself that our friendship was becoming too close, that it was dangerous for both of us because of my past. I've been trying to make up my mind to leave for almost a year."

"What's stopped you?" she asked, fear rushing through her.

"You. Every time I made up my mind to leave, the thought of not seeing you again...it tore me apart."

"And now?" she pressed.

"It would be safer for you if I did go. Those who have found me here are ruthless people, and I can't risk that more will come."

More will come. She marked his words and instinctively knew that meant that he had already killed the man who had been targeting her. She shuddered, but didn't feel the revulsion she expected to. Then again, why would she? It wasn't like he hadn't killed to protect her before.

"Don't go," she whispered. "I couldn't stand that."

"All I've brought into your life is danger and pain."

She shook her head fiercely. "That's not true. You've brought friendship and joy. You've helped me conquer my fears and live a fuller life. I have real friends, close friends, for the first time in my life and that's all because of you. Everything we've been through together, I wouldn't trade that for all the safety in the world."

And she realized that she meant that. Once upon a time being safe was the only thing that had ever mattered to her. Jeremiah had slowly changed that, helped her be more daring, bold. Maybe that was because when she was with him she actually felt safe in a way that she hadn't felt since her sister's death. She trusted him to make sure she was alright. She couldn't go back to the way things used to be.

She wouldn't.

"That's kind of you to say."

"No, it isn't. It's selfish and true."

"Dear, sweet Cindy, you are many things and selfish certainly isn't one of them," he said with a sad smile.

She was losing him. She could feel it. It was as though she could already see him packing up his things, slipping off into the night without a word, or a forwarding address.

He'd probably even have a new name so she could never find him again.

Panic seized her and she reached out and grabbed his hand. She realized hers was beginning to shake uncontrollably. "Don't you dare leave," she half-pleaded, half-demanded.

"But it would be for your-"

"If you say for my own good or my protection, I swear, I will hit you in the head with a frying pan until I knock some sense into you." She could hear the desperation in her own voice, could hear it cracking, and knew she was on the verge of tears.

"I thought women were supposed to hit men with rolling pins," he said.

"Yeah, well I have no idea if you own a rolling pin, but I know exactly where the frying pan is," she said.

She felt like she was losing it, talking nonsense. It was as though if she stopped talking, stopped trying, he'd already be gone.

"You can't go. It wouldn't be for my good or my protection. At least be honest about that. If you leave, it's because you want to, because you're the one only thinking of himself."

She saw the muscles in his arms tense and knew she had struck a nerve. He started to pull his hand away and she lunged forward and grabbed his face, holding it between both her hands. She stared into his eyes.

"Don't you dare leave, Jeremiah, whatever your name is. If you disappear on me I will never, ever forgive you."

She was crying now. Her throat seared with pain and salty tears flowed down her cheeks and onto her lips. She was shaking even harder than she had been moments before. It felt like her entire world hinged on whatever he was going to say next.

"Why do you care so much?" he asked.

She stared at him, wondering how he could ask such a question. "You're an idiot," she finally said. Her heart was pounding painfully in her chest and she felt dizzy.

"Maybe I am, but you didn't answer my question."

"Because...because I...I care about you. You're my best friend." It wasn't what she wanted to say, but it was still the truth.

He took her hands and pulled them gently down away from his face. He looked at her with an expression she couldn't quite make out. He stood abruptly. "Be that as it may you would be safer without me around."

She felt as though he had just slapped her. "Coward!" she hissed, staring up at him in fear and anger.

He blinked as his face contorted slightly. "What did you call me?"

"I called you a coward. Just because life is getting complicated you're going to cut and run."

"No one has ever dared call me that," he said, his face flushing angrily.

"Get used to it. If your answer to difficulties is to just leave them behind." She was hurt and she was lashing out. It was wrong, all wrong. This wasn't what she wanted to be saying to him, but she couldn't stop herself. The words just poured out of her, fueled by her own anguish. She took a deep breath and flung one final accusation. "Maybe that's why they kicked you out of the Mossad."

And in a flash she realized that had been the exact wrong thing to say. His face contorted into a look of fury more frightening than anything she had ever seen. She had learned to face down murderers and serial killers, but nothing could have prepared her for the terror she suddenly felt. He leaned down so that his face was mere inches from hers.

"Running away from difficulties was never my problem," he snarled. "My problem was in knowing when to leave something alone. As you can see, I still have that problem since I am here instead of gone like I should have been. Not knowing when to walk away is my weakness. It's time I got over that."

He turned and strode to the front door. He yanked it open and then slammed it shut behind him.

Cindy slumped down, her cheek hitting the surface of the table as sobs wracked her body. How had that gone so wrong? A moment later she felt something pressing against her leg and realized it was Captain, Jeremiah's German Shepherd. The dog was whining deep in his throat and he laid his head down on her knee. She dropped her hand to pet his head.

"I'm sorry, boy," she whispered to him.

She didn't know how long she sat there, waiting, wondering when or even if Jeremiah was coming back. She felt like she was going to be sick as waves of grief continued to wash over her.

Finally she dragged herself to her feet. Captain jumped toward the door and she took him outside for a minute before coming back in.

She needed to talk to Jeremiah. They couldn't leave things the way they had. His car was still in the driveway so wherever he had gone, he had walked. He lived close enough to the synagogue that he could have gone there. Personally she wouldn't mind heading over to the church and spending some quiet time in the sanctuary praying. God was the only one she really cared to talk to at that moment. Besides, Geanie and Joseph were off on their honeymoon and Mark and Traci were leaving for their well-earned vacation in Tahiti. God was the only one left she could confide in.

She got in her car and soon found herself in a long line of cars waiting to turn onto the street where the church and the synagogue were located. There seemed to be a massive traffic jam which was more than a little unusual. After spending five minutes inching forward she turned on the radio, wondering if there would be a traffic report that would let her know what was going on.

After a few seconds the song that was playing ended and an announcer came on air. "The top story this afternoon has been gubernatorial candidate Henry White's visit to Pine Springs, the latest stop on his famous walking tour of the entire state of California. Hundreds of supporters flocked to First Shepherd church where White held an impromptu rally this afternoon."

Cindy groaned to herself. That explained the traffic. All the craziness was happening at her church. It sounded like a last minute set-up which was why she hadn't heard about it. She had spent the last week under police protection leading up to Geanie and Joseph's wedding and hadn't had a chance to hear anything that was going on. She wondered what kind of logistical nightmare the event had been for everyone else.

Henry White was campaigning early and hard and he had made a big deal about getting to know the people of the entire state, not just the handful of major cities. To that end he had started weeks ago at the northern tip of the state and he was literally walking down it and would be ending it eventually in San Diego. As publicity stunts went it seemed to be working. He was the only candidate whose name she even recognized.

Cindy sighed. She hated politics and every inch of her was screaming to keep clear of the entire mess. However, she still wanted to speak with Jeremiah and she still thought the synagogue was the best place to look for him. The flow of cars on the main road seemed to gradually thin out until finally everyone who had been waiting in line with her was able to turn. She hit open road with a feeling of relief and pressed down on the accelerator a little harder than she should.

When she finally turned into the church parking lot there were only half a dozen cars still there. She glanced in her rearview mirror as she parked the car and cringed as she saw her own reflection. She usually wasn't vain about her appearance, but even she drew the line at showing her face in public when it was blatantly obvious that she had been crying.

She sat for a moment, debating what to do. There were a couple of cars in the parking lot next door by the synagogue. If Jeremiah was there she didn't want to risk running into any of his staff or congregation looking like this. His secretary already didn't like Cindy.

The church had bathrooms close to the entrance gate which was still open. She could duck in there for a minute and at least wash her face so she looked a bit more presentable. Hopefully no one she knew would see her.

She took one last quick look around before exiting her car and making a beeline for the gates. Just inside she turned to the right and grabbed hold of the door to the women's restroom. She yanked it open, stepped inside, and froze in her tracks.

A woman was sprawled on the bathroom floor, eyes frozen wide in terror. Blood had trickled out of the corner of her mouth. A great deal more of it was pooled on the floor underneath her.

Crouched above her was a man in a dark suit. There was blood on his hands. He jerked his head up as Cindy gasped. She took a hasty step backward and shouted for help even as she realized that the man who was staring up at her was Henry White.

Jeremiah was in a foul mood and he realized that coming to the synagogue might have been a tactical mistake. There had been some kind of event going on next door at the church and some of the cars had spilled over into the synagogue's parking lot. Other than that, though, there didn't seem to be anyone at the synagogue itself. That was a good thing, because he realized he was likely to tear the head off the first person he came across whether they deserved it or not.

How had everything gone so wrong? He had anticipated a number of different reactions from Cindy, played scenarios endlessly in his head for hours before she got to his house. He hadn't planned for what had actually happened and he was still reeling from the fight. His carefully ordered world was in complete chaos.

Like it or not, Cindy had gotten under his skin, pierced his armor. That was the only reason he had lost his temper. He had been hurt and angry and more than a little frightened of what he was feeling. A sworn enemy could have taunted and tortured him for hours and never caused him to lose control as he did from just a few choice words from her.

The sound of scores of car engines starting up pierced the darkness of his thoughts. Whatever was happening next door it must be breaking up. He closed his eyes and leaned his forehead into his hands. He tried to pray or think and didn't have much luck with either. At last everything seemed to quiet down outside. Quiet was good. He needed some quiet to think, regain his equilibrium.

A couple of minutes passed and the walls felt like they were closing in on him. He knew it was just because he was feeling trapped. *What is it they say? Between a rock and a hard place.*

He got up to leave, locking the door behind him. Hopefully some fresh air would help speed up the process. Once in the parking lot he noticed that there were only a handful of cars still parked in the two parking lots. He froze when he recognized one of them as Cindy's.

What was she doing here?

He stood for a moment, debating whether or not to go look for her. He really didn't want to continue their conversation in public. He wasn't sure though if waiting much longer would do either of them any good, though. He stood, unable to decide what to do.

In the distance he heard sirens and he shook himself. He turned and started to walk back toward home. He definitely couldn't continue this with her in public and at the moment he wasn't sure if he'd be able to control what he said when he saw her. He was even less sure of what she might say.

He registered that the sirens were getting louder and that there were multiple vehicles. Some accident somewhere maybe?

He had gone another dozen steps when he realized that the sirens were practically right on top of him. He turned just in time to see two police cars chasing an ambulance into the church parking lot.

A feeling of dread filled him. Cindy. Had something happened to her? He watched as the vehicles came to a stop. Paramedics and officers rushed toward the open church gate.

Jeremiah sprinted forward, praying that nothing had happened to her. As he neared the church gate he could tell that all the activity seemed to be happening just inside it.

He had almost reached the gate when a uniformed officer he didn't recognize stepped in front of him and held up a hand. "Hold it right there, sir. This is a crime scene, I need you to back up."

"I can't, you don't understand. My...friend is in there."

"I'm sorry, you're going to have to wait back here."

"I have to know if she's okay. She's a young woman, brown hair."

The officer grimaced briefly and Jeremiah's heart plunged. "Get out of my way," he growled, ready to tear the man apart.

Then just over the man's shoulder he caught sight of Liam, Mark's new partner. Before he could call to him the man shifted a step to the side and he saw that Liam was talking to Cindy.

He closed his eyes for a moment as relief flooded him. He had to get control of himself.

"What happened after you found him with the body?" he clearly heard Liam ask.

"I shouted for help and that's when Christopher here came running. He was the one who called 911," Cindy said, indicating a tall, well-dressed man with blond hair who was standing next to her.

Jeremiah took a step backward, feeling as though he had been physically struck. Cindy had been shouting for help and he hadn't heard her. Someone else had come to her rescue when it should have been him. He felt a sudden, intense hatred for Christopher, whoever he was, and imagined himself snapping the other man's neck like it was a twig.

"Hey, buddy, are you okay?" the uniformed officer asked him.

Liam glanced around. "Jeremiah, how do you fit into all of this?" the detective asked.

Jeremiah took a deep breath. "I guess I don't," he said.

"Sorry. I thought the two of you were inseparable."

Jeremiah met Cindy's eyes. From the sounds of things she had found another dead body and maybe even the murderer. Yet, somehow, all the drama was actually between the two of them and noone knew it.

He was losing control, emotions roiling within him and it was just a matter of time before he did something he'd regret. For the second time in his life he felt like everything was slipping away from him.

"I was glad I heard her shouting," Christopher said, and he put an arm around Cindy's shoulders. "I can't imagine what might have happened if I hadn't shown up."

"Take your hand off of her," Jeremiah snarled.

"Okay, settle-" the uniformed officer choked on his words as Jeremiah grabbed his hand, gave it a sharp twist, and put him on the ground.

Jeremiah stepped over him and met Christopher's startled eyes. The other man hastily backed away from Cindy, eyes widening in fear. He should be afraid. Christopher would regret trying to replace him.

"Jeremiah, stop!" Cindy said sharply.

He paused and turned to look at her. Her eyes were wide, too, but in surprise instead of fear. The others were right to fear him, but Cindy wasn't afraid of him. She never

14

was. Even if she should be. Her blind trust in him had always worried him. What would she say if she knew the truth about him?

He blinked, coming slowly out of the fog that had seemed to descend over him. She did know the truth. At least, part of it. And she was still looking at him the same way. No fear. No suspicion. Just trust.

He took a deep breath and she reached out and touched his arm. He turned to Liam. "I'm sorry. I was just so worried about her."

Liam was staring from Jeremiah to the officer he had put on the ground. "Remind me never to get in between you two," he muttered.

Jeremiah flushed. He turned and helped the officer to his feet. The man glared at him, but didn't say anything. Jeremiah knew he was lucky the man wasn't making an issue of it. He had, after all, just physically assaulted a police officer. In the man's eyes, though, Jeremiah saw fear. The man was afraid to push it.

Before anyone could do or say anything else a woman in an expensive looking blue suit hurried up, blond curls bouncing against her shoulders. "Where's my husband?" she asked in an anguished voice. Her gaze flitted to Christopher and then quickly back to the rest of them.

"Marjorie, I'm over here," a distraught voice called out.

Jeremiah tilted his head to the side. There, sitting about fifteen feet away on the ground with a police officer standing over him, was a man who looked familiar. His dark hair was cropped close and he wore suit slacks with a dress shirt and tie. The edges of the shirt as well as his hands were covered in blood.

Marjorie took a step in his direction, but Liam grabbed her arm. "I'm sorry, ma'am, you can't go over there right now."

"But that's my husband," she said, anger flaring in her eyes. "Don't you know who I am?"

"Yes, ma'am. I know who both of you are," Liam said. "And I'm going to have to insist. I need to take your statement. Where have you been for the last half hour?"

She looked taken aback. "As soon as the rally finished the driver took me to the hotel. I'd only just been there a couple of minutes when I got a phone call that something had happened to Henry. I came straight back as fast as I could."

Henry. The name clicked with the face and Jeremiah realized that the man sitting on the ground was Henry White, a politician running for governor of the state. He glanced sharply at Cindy. What exactly had she stumbled into the middle of this time?

Cindy was struggling to keep herself focused which was turning out to be an impossible task. There had been a moment where she had been absolutely sure that Jeremiah was going to kill Christopher, the man who had come when she shouted. It seemed absurd and she couldn't imagine why. Christopher was a stranger to her, and presumably to Jeremiah as well. What on earth could have set him off like that?

Maybe like her he was still on edge from their earlier conversation. Their very much *unfinished* conversation. She tried to give him a reassuring smile to calm him down, but his attention was even more scattered than hers and she wasn't sure if he actually saw it.

She took a deep breath and struggled to clear her head. Jeremiah and she could hash things out later. Now, she needed to focus on what was happening around her and what Liam was saying. She was, after all, the one who had found the body and the initial suspect.

When she had seen Henry White in the bathroom, leaning over that girl's body she had been sure he had murdered her. She had backed away as fast as she could, shouting to bring others so he wouldn't just come after her to kill her, too, to keep it quiet.

Henry hadn't moved, though. He hadn't come after her. He had just stared at her with the vacant, glassy eyes of someone in shock. Even when Christopher had come running up Henry hadn't left his spot on the bathroom floor. In fact, he hadn't left it until the officer who was now standing guard over him had arrived. The man had nearly had to pick him up physically to get him to leave the girl's side. When the policeman had half-walked, half-carried him by Cindy she had taken a good look at the politician's face.

He looked like someone in a trance. She imagined that she must have looked very similar the first time she had found a body which had also been on church grounds. No, every time she glanced over at him she couldn't believe that he was faking that reaction.

If he had killed her, it couldn't have been premeditated, she was certain of it. In fact, she was pretty certain he couldn't be the killer at all. Maybe she was just empathizing with him because she'd had an experience that she viewed as similar. She needed to look at things more objectively. Politicians were notorious for being able to lie to the world and hide their true faces. Plus, after all, she had found them in the women's room. What on earth had he been doing in there?

Maybe when Liam questioned him, he'd find out. It seemed like Henry hadn't said a word until calling out to his wife just a minute before. Liam was questioning her now and she seemed very agitated. Then again, who wouldn't be?

"Who called to tell you that something had happened to your husband?" Liam asked.

"His campaign organizer, Geoffrey Wells," Marjorie said.

"And how exactly did he find out?" Liam asked.

"Um, that would be me," Christopher said, looking sheepish. "I'm one of the campaign staffers and after I called 911, I called Geoffrey."

Cindy nodded. "I know he called someone after calling 911 and told them to hurry down here because there had been an 'incident'." She put emphasis on the word because even at the time it had seemed far too mild a word to describe what had happened.

Liam looked around. "So, where is Geoffrey Wells?"

Marjorie and Christopher looked around as well. "I don't see him," Marjorie admitted. "I know he was on his way to a meeting after the rally."

"Is there a reason both of you left before Henry?" Liam asked.

Marjorie shook her head. "Almost everyone but a couple of staffers leave these things before Henry. He insists on staying as late as possible to shake hands and answer questions. He doesn't leave until the last voter does, sometimes hours after an event is over. By then I'll have gotten some rest, be changed for dinner and ready to talk over the day with him. Geoffrey is busy coordinating and setting up the next event the moment one ends. None of us has time to stay as long as Henry. But that's his job. To be accessible to the voters. At least, that's how he sees it."

"You don't agree?" Cindy asked before she could stop herself.

Liam glanced at her out of the corner of his eyes, shaking his head slightly.

"I think he gives too much of himself. He ends each day so exhausted he can barely stand. And there's weeks to go before this tour is over. Even then he won't be able to take a rest. Not until the election."

"Okay, so who was still here with your husband when you left?" Liam asked.

Marjorie shrugged. "A lot of people. I don't know. I'm sorry."

"We were just getting ready to leave actually," Christopher volunteered. "It was just him, a couple other staffers, and me. I was getting ready to call the guy to come lock up after us. I always stay on site with Henry so I'm responsible for making sure buildings get locked behind us."

"Do you know the victim?" Liam asked.

Cindy turned so she could look at Christopher while he was talking. Out of the corner of her eye she could see Jeremiah standing, arms folded across his chest. He looked slightly calmer, but not much.

"No. I think I might have seen her, though."

"At the rally?"

"No, a couple of days ago. Different rally, different city. I can't be sure, though. I'm sorry."

"Her name was Lydia Jenkins. The name familiar?" Liam asked.

Christopher shook his head.

"How about you?" Liam asked, turning to Marjorie.

"No, I've never heard the name," she said.

Liam was doing a great job, but Cindy couldn't help but wish that Mark was there. He and Traci should be en route to Tahiti, though. Liam was a good detective from everything she had seen, but she'd feel so much better with Mark on the case.

"She's not a member of the church," Cindy offered.

Liam turned to her. "You know, I've got your preliminary statement. If you want to head home I can swing by later and get more details."

She shook her head. "That's okay. I'll stay."

She glanced at Jeremiah. "You can go if you want. I'll be okay."

Cindy saw the muscle in his jaw clench and she realized in surprise that somehow what she had just said had made him angry. She couldn't figure out how it possibly could have, but didn't have time to fixate on it. She knew from experience that she was going to be at the heart of this murder investigation whether she wanted to be or not, and she didn't want to miss a word of what Liam and the others were saying. The smallest thing could end up being important later.

"I'll stay," Jeremiah said, his voice curt.

"Okay," she replied, not knowing what else she could say. That seemed to be the wrong thing, too, because she saw him scowl.

Liam moved over to stand next to Henry and Cindy followed. "Sir, can you tell me what happened?" Liam asked.

"I was heading to the parking lot," Henry said, his voice shaky. "I heard...I thought I heard a woman scream. I ran, but didn't see anyone in the parking lot. I realized maybe it was coming from somewhere else. I saw the women's restroom. It was the closest door in the building, and I yanked it open."

He paused and put his head in his hands for a moment. Cindy took a step backward, wondering if he was going to be sick. When he lifted his head again, his skin was sickly colored. His hands were shaking now. "I saw her on the floor. I ran over to see if I could help. There was blood. And she was just staring...staring. I think she was dead."

He glanced over at Cindy. "Then she came in."

"How much time had passed?" Liam asked.

"I really don't know. A minute. Five. She was just staring...and I couldn't wake her...and I didn't know what to do."

Cindy's heart went out to him. She remembered finding her first dead body. Time had lost meaning for her as well.

"Did you know her?" Liam asked.

He shook his head. "I saw her at a couple of rallies. She never came up to me or shook my hand. She always hung back. I don't know who she was, but noone deserves...that."

Tears sprung to his eyes, and Cindy's heart ached for him.

Mark leaned his head back against his seat and squeezed Traci's hand. They had just taken their seats in the first class cabin.

"Tahiti," she said excitedly.

"Tahiti," he breathed. "And you."

"It's probably our last trip together alone for a while."

He squeezed her hand harder. "I still can't believe we're having a baby."

"September 18th."

"How often do babies arrive on their actual due date?"

"I don't know. That's why I packed a few books for you to read on vacation. You know, *What to Expect When You're Expecting*. That kind of thing."

He chuckled. "Never thought I'd say this, but I'm looking forward to reading them."

"We're going to be okay."

"We're going to be better than okay," he said. "We're going to be great."

He stretched out his legs. "I don't think I'll ever be able to fly coach again."

She laughed. "I was just thinking the same thing."

"Great minds think alike."

"I keep wondering what trouble everyone's going to get into while we're gone," she mused.

"I keep trying not to think about that. Whatever it is, I'm sure they can survive two weeks without us."

In the back of his head there was a little nagging doubt. He tried very hard not to think about the news Cindy had given him that morning that pertained to his deceased partner, the man he had known as Paul but who was really someone else entirely.

As the plane pulled away from the gate he took a deep breath. Two weeks with just the two of them on an island. It was going to be wonderful. It was exactly what they both needed.

"Did you remember to turn off your phone?" Traci asked as flight attendants began to do their safety spiel.

He turned and grinned at her. "I didn't even bring it."

She raised her eyebrows in mock surprise. "But, what if something important happens, someone needs to reach us?"

"Nothing is more important than the two of us and uninterrupted quality time. Besides, if the world ends I'm sure someone on the island will let us know."

Cindy was sitting on the ground next to Henry, talking to him occasionally while Liam finished his interviews with everyone else. The man was still in shock but doing a whole lot better. Jeremiah had glared at her when she sat down next to him. He probably didn't think it was safe. He probably thought Henry was the murderer. She was pretty sure Liam thought that.

Eventually Jeremiah had stalked off. She wasn't sure where he had gone. For all she knew he was at the synagogue or even back home. Sylvia, the business manager at the church, had been called. It was her number Christopher had had. She had unlocked the facilities earlier and stayed during setup but had to leave before the rally got underway.

She had pulled Cindy aside for a minute when she got there, muttering under her breath about how people were going to start calling First Shepherd the "Murder Church". Cindy had told her briefly what had happened before Sylvia went off to talk with Liam.

Night had fallen but Sylvia had turned on some extra lights other than the handful that normally came on at dusk. Cindy pulled her phone out of her pocket to check the time. Mark and Traci should be on their flight. Half a dozen times she had been tempted to call him, but she wasn't going to be the one to potentially spoil a vacation the two of them desperately needed. Besides, Liam was doing just fine. There wasn't anything more Mark could have done.

She wondered how much longer it would be until Liam was finished. She knew from experience that when officers took your statement they asked you dozens of questions several different ways, trying to jog loose extra details or things you might not have thought to bring up before. It made the process incredibly thorough but also agonizingly slow.

Christopher wandered over and crouched down next to them. "I don't think we'll be here much longer," he said. "The detective said he was done with me. I'll stay, of course, until everyone's free to go...or, whatever."

He flushed and she gathered that he was wondering if his boss was about to be arrested. Given the state in which he had been found, she was sure that his status was the only thing that had kept him from being arrested immediately.

"What a mess," Christopher muttered, rubbing his eyes with his hand.

He looked tired and strained. Cindy was feeling better than she could have expected. She had a sneaking suspicion that was because dealing with a murder was less stressful than the thought of resuming her conversation with Jeremiah.

Sad, but true, she thought to herself.

She heard a step and glanced up just as a camera light flashed in her face. She shouted and Christopher jumped to his feet. The officer who had been standing nearby facing the other direction whirled around.

Cindy blinked furiously, but all she could see were bright spots.

"This is a crime scene, get back!" she heard the officer shout.

There was another flash of light and another followed by excited voices yelling all at the same time.

"How did they find out?" Henry asked.

"Who? What's going on?" Cindy asked.

"The vultures have arrived," he said, voice miserable.

"Who?"

"The press," Christopher said.

Cindy scrambled to her feet, her vision clearing as she watched some officers pushing back half a dozen people.

"That's just the first wave. The rest will be arriving soon," Christopher said, anger flaring in his voice. "We need to get out of here."

A hand descended on Cindy's shoulder and she spun around with a gasp. Jeremiah was standing behind her, features tense. She had no idea where he'd come from. "Come with me," he said, voice low.

She nodded and let him guide her deeper into the church grounds away from the reporters.

"The last thing we need is our picture with that guy on the front of every paper and news site come morning," he said grimly.

His avoidance of publicity finally made perfect sense to her. He might have a different name than he used to, but he would still look the same. Maybe he was afraid of being recognized.

"We can wait in here," she said, fishing her keys out of her purse and unlocking one of the Sunday School rooms.

They walked inside, closed the door and then sat down at one of the tables. Jeremiah took a deep breath. "Okay, start at the beginning."

She noticed that he sounded more like himself, the accent having faded into the background again. She wondered if that meant he was calmer, or at least more in control of himself than he had been earlier.

His request irritated her. If he'd been paying attention he would have heard her explain it to Liam half a dozen times already. Still, he had been agitated. Besides, it was good to go over it again, make sure there wasn't a shred of information she had forgotten to share earlier.

"Well, I finally decided to come look for you instead of waiting at your house any longer," she started.

A grimace crossed his face for a moment and then was gone. The sudden urge to tell him this was all his fault was great, but she managed not to.

"I figured I'd see if you were at the synagogue. By the time I made it over here with all the traffic from the rally letting out I decided to use the restroom and wash my face so it wasn't immediately obvious that I had been crying."

She paused and was rewarded when he flinched slightly.

"So, I headed to the women's room that's there close to the gate. I opened the door and I saw the dead woman with Henry crouched over her. I backed out, shouting for help. I heard someone running toward me and, to be honest, I really thought it was you."

A new expression passed over his face very briefly and was gone. She wasn't sure what it was he was feeling, but the look she had just seen was chilling.

"It wasn't, though. It was Christopher. He asked me what was wrong. I told him to call 911 because a woman was dead in the bathroom and there was a man in there with her. He did. Then he opened the door, recognized Henry and called to him. Henry didn't move though. We kept the door open, watching him to make sure he didn't try to destroy evidence or anything."

"That was incredibly foolish," Jeremiah said. "What if he'd tried to attack you?"

"I realized that if he was going to try, he would have done it when he first saw me. The guy was in shock, really out of it. And with Christopher there I felt safe."

Again that expression flashed across Jeremiah's face. Was it anger? That didn't feel quite right. It couldn't be jealousy, could it? That just seemed ridiculous.

"Anyway, a patrol car arrived first and an officer had to practically carry Henry out of there. Then Liam arrived and you were there for the rest."

He nodded.

"I don't think Henry did it."

"All evidence to the contrary," Jeremiah said.

"I know how it looks. I mean, goodness, I'm the one who found him that way. He was in shock, though."

"Could be the reality of what he'd done finally hit him."

"I don't think so. He doesn't seem like a killer to me."

Jeremiah raised an eyebrow. "Not everyone who is seems like it."

She stared at him for a long minute and she saw him finally begin to squirm. A thousand retorts rushed through her mind. In the end, though, he was right. She couldn't always spot a killer. Life the last couple years would have been so much easier if she could.

"I just don't see it," she finally said.

"He is a politician. Lying comes naturally to them."

"Yeah, but I would have thought that by that same logic he would have been a lot smarter if he did want to kill her.

I mean, he could have hired someone or at least planned it where he wouldn't be found with the body."

"Maybe it was an accident or a heat of the moment thing."

Cindy crossed her arms over her chest. "The woman looked like she had been stabbed. I'm pretty sure the police didn't find any weapons in that bathroom."

Cindy's phone rang and she reached into her purse to grab it.

"Hello?"

"Cindy, Liam."

"Oh, hi, Liam," she said so Jeremiah would know who she was talking to.

"Where are you?"

"Jeremiah and I retreated to one of the Sunday school rooms when the press showed up."

"Sensible. We're working on clearing them out of here now."

"Do you have more questions for me?" she asked.

"Not at the moment, but then again, I know how to get hold of you."

"Are you arresting Henry?" she asked.

There was a pause. Finally Liam said, "We're taking him to the precinct to ask him more questions. That's all I can say."

She rolled her eyes. Mark would have given her more information. Maybe she would drop by the precinct later to see Liam and make sure he had everything he needed from her. Then she could try to get more information from him.

"Let me know when it's safe to leave," she said.

"It should be in a few minutes. If you are accosted by any members of the press, I'd greatly appreciate it if you didn't tell them anything."

"I won't," she promised.

"Jeremiah either."

"I can guarantee you that Jeremiah won't say anything to the press," she said.

Jeremiah nodded agreement.

"Thank you. I have to go."

He hung up and she returned the phone to her purse.

"He wasn't very helpful."

"You know, Cindy, you don't have to get involved. It's not up to you to solve this mystery."

"But I want to," she said. It was true. She wasn't sure when the need to solve mysteries had taken over. She was sure, though, that solving this one would give her something to think about other than the conversation she and Jeremiah had had earlier.

He sighed. "Fine, but be smart about it and careful. Liam might like you, but he's not Mark and with Mark away we don't know exactly what he'll do or how much of a hard line he'll take about interference."

"I know, but with Mark gone, he's definitely going to need an extra set of eyes trying to figure things out."

"How can you be so sure Henry is innocent?"

"I can't explain it other than I felt like I could relate to him," Cindy said.

"You know setting himself up like that, almost like someone was framing him, would be the smart move for a politician to make," he pointed out.

"Yeah, but as far as I can tell there hasn't been a hint of scandal around him at all. Why create some?"

"Publicity?" he suggested.

She shook her head. "I hate politics and even I know who he is thanks to his Walk Campaign."

Jeremiah pulled his phone out of his pocket and fiddled with it for a minute. He nodded, apparently having found what it was he was looking for.

"Well?" she asked.

"The Walk campaign came about because Henry said that the problem with politicians was twofold. First, that they had never walked a mile in their constituents' shoes and second, that they only seemed to know or care about the needs of a few parts of the state while ignoring the vast majority of it. He asked how anyone could hope to govern the state without understanding it and the problems faced by all its inhabitants. When a rival challenged him to prove that he was any different, he declared that he was going to walk down the length of the entire state so that he could meet people from different areas and hear their concerns firsthand."

"He started up north, so he's come a long ways already," she said.

"Ambitious. And you're right, it has gotten him a lot of publicity and notoriety. He's speaking about the troubles in the state and how they're going to get worse if we don't take a stand and face them head on. The farther he walks the more the polls seem to be swinging in his favor."

"Which could explain why someone would be interested in framing him for murder," Cindy said.

Jeremiah shook his head. "If he was being framed, don't you think the real killer would have left the murder weapon somewhere nice and conspicuous?"

It was a good point, but she didn't want to admit it.

Jeremiah returned his eyes to his screen, clearly reading up more on the politician while she studied her hands. She just couldn't believe that the stricken man she had seen had killed that poor woman.

The question was, who could have? The man was sure to have enemies, political ones at the very least.

Her phone rang again and she wondered if it was Liam telling them that the coast was clear. She pulled her phone out of her purse and glanced at the screen.

"It's my father. He never calls," she said. Warning bells began to go off in her head and her stomach lurched.

Jeremiah looked up sharply as she answered the phone.

"Hey, Dad," she said, the breath catching in her throat. "What's going on?"

"Honey, you better sit down," he said.

"Why? What's happened?" she asked.

There was a long pause before he finally answered. "It's Kyle."

The phone slipped from Cindy's hand and clattered to the ground. She was white as a ghost as she swayed for a moment on her feet and then sat down on a chair.

"What happened?" he asked.

She didn't say anything.

He scooped up her phone and pressed it to his ear. "Hello?"

"Who is this?" her father asked.

"Jeremiah. I'm a friend of Cindy's. She just dropped her phone. She's sitting down now. What's going on?"

"There's been an accident. Her brother Kyle is hurt pretty badly. We don't know more than that yet, but...it's not looking good," he said, his voice cracking.

"Where's he at?"

"St. Mary's Hospital in Las Vegas."

"Okay. I'll see that Cindy gets there," Jeremiah said.

"Thank you. Kyle told us you were a good man. We are just getting on a plane..." he drifted off.

"We'll all be praying for him," Jeremiah said.

"Thank you."

Cindy's father hung up and Jeremiah placed the phone down on the table next to her. "He's in the hospital in Vegas," he said softly.

She nodded, but didn't say anything.

"If we leave now we can drive there in five hours," he said.

"It will be faster if I fly," she said, seemingly snapping out of it as she grabbed her phone. "They should have a flight leaving soon."

"You should grab some stuff from home."

She shook her head. "No time."

"Do you want me to go with you?" he asked.

"No. My parents can get weird when things are stressful. I don't need that right now. We don't need that."

He didn't like the answer, but he understood. Cindy's relationship with her parents was a bit strained, at least from her point of view. If having him there with them was going to stress her out more then he could stay away.

"Can I drive you to the airport? I don't think you should drive yourself."

"Yes, please."

Cautiously they left the Sunday school room, Cindy locking the door behind them. They walked slowly back toward the crime scene and Jeremiah listened intently to see how many people might still be around.

It was fairly quiet, though, and a few seconds later they discovered why. Only a couple of police officers seemed to be left. The witnesses, the suspect, Liam, and the press all appeared to be gone.

Jeremiah felt momentary relief and they continued quickly on to Cindy's car. She wordlessly handed him the keys and climbed into the passenger's side.

A minute later they were on the road and there was silence as Cindy searched for and bought her ticket. When she was finished she leaned her head back against the seat for a moment, eyes closed. A couple minutes passed before she straightened back up and called the business manager at the church to let her know what was happening. The call took less than a minute but her voice was cracking with emotion by the end of it.

They drove on for a few more minutes in silence. Finally Jeremiah couldn't take it anymore. "Do you know what Kyle was doing in Vegas?"

Cindy's brother was the host of a television travel show for the adventurous and was always doing things that seemed incredibly dangerous. He was Cindy's opposite in so many ways and their parents' favorite. He knew all that added to her frustrations with him and her friction with her parents. A lot of healing had taken place a few months back, though, between Cindy and Kyle on an adventure trip that he had roped them into taking.

"I honestly don't know. Mom usually tells me when he's out shooting a new episode but she never said anything about Vegas."

"I see."

She closed her eyes and leaned her head back again. He figured that was the end of conversation for the drive. A moment later he realized he was wrong.

"How did you come to work for the Mossad?" she asked.

He cleared his throat. "As you know, everyone in Israel spends a couple of years in the military doing service. During my training period I caught the attention of the right person who thought that my time and skills were better put to other uses."

"They recruited you."

"Yes, you can say that. My zeal for both G-d and country made it imperative that I say yes. To serve one's country in that way is a high calling."

"And yet you're no longer with them."

"That is correct."

"Why?"

That was a question he was most certainly not answering. It went straight to the heart of all the things that he wouldn't, couldn't tell her. He didn't want to lie to her, but there was no way he could tell her the truth.

"They decided that it was time for me to retire."

She opened her eyes and turned to look at him.

"I thought spies didn't retire."

"What do you think, they kill you when you've outlived your usefulness?"

"I don't know."

"You've seen too many movies," he said with a shake of his head.

"So, what happens when you retire?" she asked.

"Well, in my case, change of name, change of country, change of job."

"So what, they just made you a rabbi and dropped you in California, waved and said 'good luck'?"

"It's a bit more complex than that."

"Explain it to me."

"I started training when I was young to someday be a rabbi. The day I entered the army I was intending to resume my studies when I got out. When I...retired...I was sent to America to a state back east. I lived with what you might think of as a foster family who helped me to acclimate to my new life while I studied. They didn't know my name or anything about me, but they helped me adjust and fit in. Then one day a man arrived with a package for me. My new identity. I moved out west the next morning and was able to obtain the rabbi position at the synagogue in Pine Springs."

36

"And then two years later we met," she said softly.

"Yes."

"And things got crazy."

"That's one way of putting it."

"So, what happens now?" she asked.

"What do you mean?" he said, partly to stall for time and partly to make sure he understood what she was asking.

"When I come back home in a few days are you still going to be here or will you have gone without so much as a goodbye?"

"I promise you I will not leave without saying goodbye."

Out of the corner of his eye he saw her hands ball into fists. Clearly she'd been hoping he would say that he wouldn't leave at all. He couldn't make that promise. Not now. Especially not since old enemies had found him and had already tried to hurt Cindy because of him.

Things with her had always been complicated. Now they were downright dangerous. Besides, there was more than just the two of them to worry about. He was also responsible for all the people at the synagogue. Who was to say old enemies wouldn't go after them as well?

Some of the last words of the man who had been trying to kill Cindy for the past several days echoed through his mind. *You never look to the left or the right.*

He had said that in response to Jeremiah not recognizing him. What did it mean, though? He felt like the meaning should be clear and yet it wasn't.

Still, just leaving like he had often thought of doing was no longer an option. Instead of trying to hunt him down again his enemies might just decide to flush him out by going after those he'd left behind. No, he was definitely staying until that threat was ended. And after that G-d alone knew what the future might hold.

"Do you need me to do anything while you're gone?" he asked, changing the subject.

"There's nothing I can think of," she said, and he could hear the strain in her voice.

At this point he didn't know which was causing her more distress, the conversation about the two of them or the fact that her brother could be dying. It was terrible timing all the way around, especially when coupled with the murder she had stumbled onto.

We just can't catch a break, he thought to himself.

They drove the rest of the way in silence. At the airport Jeremiah got out of the car and stood in front of her, searching her eyes with his. "Call when you get there, please," he said softly.

"I will," she said, dropping her eyes.

Normally he would have hugged her, but he had a feeling if he did it would make this parting harder on both of them. "And call if you need anything."

She nodded, still looking down.

"Okay," he said, forcing himself to step to the side.

She walked into the building and when she had disappeared he got in the car and started the drive back. It didn't feel right, though. He should be going with her. He knew what she had said about not wanting weirdness with her parents and that made sense, but she needed someone to be there for her during this time. Her parents had each other. Cindy needed someone who was going to be her support and comfort during this time.

But she didn't want him playing that role. At least, not today. He wished for a moment that Geanie and Joseph weren't off on their honeymoon. Either of them would have been glad to go with her. He would have trusted them both to take care of her, too.

They had all been through a lot together. Mark and Traci, too. Comrades in war. That's how he thought of them. In his old life he'd had associates, very few of whom he would have thought of as friends. What he had here with these people was on the one hand very familiar and on the other very alien.

When you passed through the fire with people, it bonded you together forever in a strange way. Even if you went your separate ways later, there was still that connection. So all of them had that connection, but they had also become friends. They were people he not only trusted but also liked. He enjoyed spending time with them even if that time was often fraught with peril. More than that, they enjoyed spending time with him.

For the first time since he was a very young boy he felt like he belonged someplace, like he had roots. For people like him that was often no more than a distant dream, a beautiful sounding life that could never be lived in the real world.

Cindy, Joseph, Geanie, Mark and Traci were family to him. That was something he thought he could never again have, and it was something he wasn't willing to give up. G-d help them all.

As she stepped foot on the plane Cindy's terror resurfaced and grabbed her by the throat, squeezing until she felt as though she couldn't breathe. She finally sank, gasping into her seat next to a window. Her hands were shaking as she shoved her purse under the seat in front of her.

Fixating on things with Jeremiah in the car had helped her keep her fear for her brother at bay. Now, though, it refused to be denied any longer. What crazy stunt had Kyle pulled this time? She'd warned him that he was going to get himself killed doing all the extreme adventure travel that he did. For so many years she had hated him for it, seeing it as being reckless and disrespectful, especially in light of what had happened to their sister when they were all kids.

Her parents had to be going out of their minds. Kyle was their favorite. Her mother in particular was constantly gushing over everything Kyle did and driving Cindy crazy while doing it. For years she'd felt like the child that didn't exist, living only in the shadows of her famous brother and her dead sister. She had slowly grown to accept that as the norm and had given up on ever impressing her mother with anything she did.

Whatever happened, she knew that the next few days were going to be hellish for all of them. She wished that Jeremiah was in the seat next to her, holding her hand and giving her the courage to face the world. She was afraid, though, of what her parents might say or do if he was with her. They had yet to meet him. They certainly didn't know that Cindy had feelings for him. Sometimes her mother could be so self-absorbed it was rude. Both of her parents could be overly blunt and even downright mean-spirited when stressed out.

She and Jeremiah simply weren't in the best place to deal with whatever her parents might dish out. Two days ago she would probably have asked him to come. That was before she knew that he had seriously considered leaving to protect her. Now the whole world was upside down and she wasn't sure where she stood even with him. She wasn't sure their relationship could survive the amount of pressure that would be put on it if he was there with her. Maybe she was just being paranoid, but there were reasons her parents didn't know any of her friends.

"Ma'am, are you alright?"

She looked up at a flight attendant. The woman was staring down at her with obvious concern.

"Not really," Cindy managed to squeak out. It was then she noticed that her breathing had seemed to accelerate. Try as she might she was having trouble catching her breath. In a panic she realized that she must be hyperventilating. "My brother...in...hospital...going to...see...him," she managed to get out.

The woman nodded sympathetically. She reached into the seat pocket and pulled out a bag. "Try breathing into this, it should help you get under control," she said. "In the meantime, is there anything I can get you?"

Cindy took the bag and shook her head. She opened it up and began breathing into it as the flight attendant moved away to help someone with their bag. The trick actually seemed to be helping and she almost had her breathing back under control when a man in a gray suit stopped next to her aisle.

He had a briefcase in one hand and a trench coat slung over his arm. He stowed both in the overhead bin and then looked at her as he took his seat on the aisle. "You can't be airsick already," he said with a smile.

She shook her head and slowly lowered the bag. "I was hyperventilating," she explained. She didn't want the man worrying that she was seconds from being sick on him.

"I understand, but you know, it's safer to travel in planes than cars," he said.

"It's not that," she said.

"Really? Because most people who look like you do before a plane takes off are afraid to fly."

"My brother's in the hospital. He might be dying. I just found out and I'm freaking out about that," she said, figuring that should put an end to his questions.

"I'm sorry," he said frowning. "That's a terrible reason to have to go to Vegas. Or anywhere for that matter."

She nodded.

"I will tell you, though. One of the best hospitals in the country, in my opinion, is in Vegas. St. Mary's."

"That's the one he's at."

"Then he's in excellent hands. You can trust me on that. I'm Martin, by the way."

"Cindy," she said. She took a closer look at him. He looked to be roughly her age. He had dark hair, blue eyes, and a nice smile. His suit was nice, but not memorable, and he was wearing a wedding ring.

He followed her gaze and smiled. "Don't worry, I'm not hitting on you. I've been married five years to the most wonderful woman in the world, and only a complete idiot would screw that up."

"I didn't-" Cindy began, embarrassed.

He waved his hand. "I'm a salesman. I spend a lot of time flying, and I quickly found that I'd rather spend that time talking to my neighbors than pretending to read or sleep. I guess I'm just a people person."

She couldn't help but smile. "I guess that's why you're a salesman."

His grin broadened. "Yes, ma'am."

Jeremiah was tired when he turned onto his street. He had spent the entire drive home worrying about Cindy. No matter how many times he tried to convince himself that she was going to be okay, he couldn't shake the feeling that something terrible was going to happen to her in Vegas. Something worse even than the potential death of her brother.

He told himself he was being paranoid, but where Cindy was concerned he had learned there was no such thing. She had the most amazing knack for finding trouble. Or, rather, trouble found her. He tried to tell himself that she was going to be fine. She was going to be with family, so she wouldn't be alone even though she might end up wishing that she was.

He was so preoccupied that it took him a moment to realize that there was a strange car parked outside his house. He slowed down before parking Cindy's car in the driveway. He got out, and noticed that there was a man standing on his porch, face hidden in the shadows.

Jeremiah tensed, preparing for anything. The man he had killed the day before at the wedding had warned him that more would be coming after him. This could be one of them.

He took a step forward, body twisted to the side so he'd make a smaller target. "Show yourself," he ordered.

The figure on the porch hesitated for a moment and then walked slowly down the stairs. When he stepped into the light from one of the street lamps Jeremiah could barely contain his surprise. It was Christopher, the man who had come to Cindy's aid earlier. The one he'd almost torn apart.

5

"What are you doing here?" Jeremiah asked suspiciously.

"I've come on behalf of Henry White," Christopher said, stepping carefully toward him with a concerned look on his face.

He was right to look concerned. Jeremiah still had an urge to snap his neck. He shoved his hands into his pockets instead. As much as he didn't want to talk with the man he realized that it would probably be a conversation better carried on inside than outside for all the world to see and hear.

"Let's talk inside," Jeremiah said, striding forward.

Christopher backed out of his way, and then followed him into the house. Once inside he sat down at the kitchen table in the same chair Cindy had been occupying a few hours before.

Captain came bounding in from the other room, stopping to stare at Christopher. The dog didn't like him either, and that fact gave Jeremiah a bit of satisfaction. Captain glanced at Jeremiah, and then turned and headed back to the bedroom.

Jeremiah leaned against the kitchen counter. "So, what does your boss want?"

"Your help, actually."

"To do what?"

"To clear his name of this murder."

Jeremiah tilted his head to the side. "I think maybe your boss has mistaken me for a police officer. That's not my job."

Christopher cleared his throat. "Yes, but for someone whose job it isn't, you seem to help people all the time."

"And just where are you getting your information?"

"From one of the police officers. He said that you and Cindy are constantly helping the detectives with their cases; that the two of you are the real heroes of the Pine Springs police force."

Jeremiah barely restrained the urge to laugh as he pictured Mark's face if he heard someone say that. "I would hardly think so. The force has fine detectives; the credit goes to them. Now, I'm busy, so if you'll just-"

"Please," Christopher said, getting to his feet. "I've been working with Henry for months. He was a friend before that. I know he couldn't have done this."

"Then I'm sure the police will clear him," Jeremiah said.

"You don't understand. Every hour that this goes unsolved, that suspicion is on him, costs votes. More than we can afford to lose. This state is sick and Henry White has the cure, but not if the people think he's a killer. I'm confident that the police will eventually figure out who really did this, but we don't have the time to waste. Anything that can be done, any fresh pair of eyes, will help tremendously. I need your help to keep a good man from having his reputation and his career ruined by someone else's crime."

"What if you're wrong and your boss is involved?"

Christopher took a deep breath. "Then the sooner he's brought to justice the better it will be for everyone else, including that girl's family."

Jeremiah had too many problems of his own to get involved, especially since the press was going to be crawling all over this mess until it was over. He shook his head. "I'm sorry, but I just can't help."

Christopher looked stricken. "I thought...Cindy said we would get to the bottom of this when I talked to her at the church."

"Cindy has some family stuff to deal with. She can't help you now either. Good luck to you," Jeremiah said, moving toward the door.

For a moment Christopher just stood where he was, and Jeremiah began to think he was going to have to throw the other man out bodily. Finally, though, Christopher walked over. Jeremiah held open the door, and as soon as the other man was outside he closed and locked it.

I'm done with you, he thought to himself.

Cindy was relieved that the plane ride was over quickly. She was also grateful to Martin for keeping her distracted for the duration of the flight. As the plane taxied to the gate he pulled a business card out of his suit pocket and handed it to her.

"If you need anything, give me a call. I'll be in town for a few days."

"Thanks," she said, pocketing the card. She wondered what it said about her and all her experiences the past couple of years that she was still slightly suspicious of his motives. She wished she wasn't, but she couldn't just dismiss out of hand the fact that killers had tried to get close to her in the past to find out what she knew.

That couldn't be the case here, though. This guy couldn't have been targeting her since she herself hadn't known she was heading to Vegas until the phone call. They had driven straight to the airport, and she'd barely made the flight.

"I'm serious now. Vegas is a hard place to be by yourself especially when you're worrying about family. If you need to talk or even just need a recommendation on a good hotel close to the hospital, let me know."

She nodded. She hadn't even thought that far in advance. She wondered where her parents were staying. She'd probably end up with them even though that thought made her shudder a bit. "I'll keep it in mind," she said to him, forcing a smile.

He nodded, seemingly satisfied. Maybe he just was a nice guy. A minute later they were parked at the gate, and she stood and shuffled toward the front of the plane with everyone else. She walked beside Martin as they headed toward baggage claim and ground transportation. She shook her head as they passed rows of slot machines. First and last chance to win for passengers coming and going. When they reached the carousels that were spewing out people's luggage, he gave her a wave before turning aside to collect his bags.

Cindy walked outside and followed the signs to the taxi stand. "St. Mary's," she told the driver.

A minute later they were away from the airport and edging into snarled traffic. Everywhere around her was the flash of neon, lighting up the night sky. Between the sea of taillights and the glaring signs she felt half-blind. Besides tons of cars on the streets, throngs of people were walking by. The city felt alive, pulsing with its own mechanized heartbeat. She couldn't help but wonder for a moment what it was like to live there. All the hurry, all the hype, and everywhere the flashing lights.

After what seemed a lifetime the driver finally turned onto a street with less traffic. Two minutes later he was pulling up outside the main entrance of the hospital.

Cindy paid him with hands that shook, and she realized her pulse was again racing out of control. She checked her phone, but there were no new messages. She had feared that her father would have called and told her that it was too late, Kyle was already dead.

She took a deep breath, got out of the cab, and marched into the hospital. She went up to the reception desk. "I'm looking for Kyle Preston," she said, her voice cracking. "I'm his sister."

The woman behind the counter gave her a pitying look that made Cindy's stomach clench fiercely. "I'm so sorry for what happened," she whispered.

Time seemed to stand still. "Is he dead?" Cindy asked, her own voice sounding like she was drawing the syllables out one minute at a time.

The woman took a deep breath. "No, but he is in the ICU."

"You didn't even have to look him up," Cindy noticed.

"Your brother has a lot of fans here," the woman said. "About a year ago while he was filming one of his shows here he ended up saving a little girl's life. He was almost drowned in the process. He's a hero."

Cindy felt her stomach clench even more, and she wanted to double over with the pain. She was beginning to sweat, and she felt like she was going to be sick. She hadn't heard about that incident. Her mom was always bragging about everything Kyle did. Apparently, though, she had been smart enough not to tell Cindy about that one.

"Which way?" she asked, her voice little more than a raw croak.

The nurse pointed to one of the hallways. "Halfway down there's an elevator. Take it to the second floor, and when you get out turn left. You'll find a check-in desk at the end of that hallway."

"Thanks," Cindy said. She headed toward the elevator, feeling like she was some sort of automaton. She could barely feel her legs, and yet they kept moving, taking her closer and closer to her brother.

Up on the second floor she found the check-in desk where the woman had said it would be. The man sitting at it gave her a sad smile. "Kyle's sister?" he asked.

She nodded, practically too numb to care how he knew that. He handed her a clipboard with a sign-in sheet.

"Just put your name down, and then I'll take you to the observation room."

She wrote out her name and handed it back to him. Then she followed him through a door after he entered his pin into the keypad next to it.

Seconds later he was escorting her into a small room that had half a dozen chairs all facing a large window. Through the window she could see into a hospital room, and she could tell that there was someone lying on a bed, surrounded by machines. Standing next to the window were her parents. Her mom's short brown hair was the same color as Cindy's. Her dad, who was a good six inches taller than both of them had black hair shot through with silver streaks. They were standing together, shoulders almost touching, unmoving like some statue dedicated to grief and vigilance.

The nurse left, and Cindy stepped farther into the room. "Hi," she said.

Both her parents jumped as though startled. Her dad turned around and strode forward quickly to hug her. "Glad you made it okay," he said. "We weren't sure when you were coming."

"I came as fast as I could," she said, realizing that she had never called them to let them know she had gotten a flight.

Her mom turned slowly and stared at her as if she wasn't really seeing her. Her blue eyes were awash with tears and her entire face was red and puffy from crying. She nodded at Cindy then turned back to the window.

When her dad released Cindy she forced herself to walk up to the window and look into the next room even though she didn't want to.

Kyle was in the hospital bed. What she could see of his face was chalk white and the rest was covered with bandages. It looked like one leg and both arms were in casts.

"Can we go in and see him?" she asked.

"No, this is as close as they'll let us," her dad said. "I think they're afraid that we'll get in the way if..."

He didn't finish his sentence, but she got the implication. If he took a turn for the worse and the doctors and nurses had to rush in. They could also be afraid of exposing him to any germs in the state he was in.

"What's wrong with him?" she asked. It had to be more than just a few broken bones.

51

"There's been internal bleeding and there's some damage to some of his organs. I...I don't remember which ones," her dad admitted.

What stupid stunt had Kyle pulled that ended like this? She had always been terrified that his recklessness would cost him. Would cost all of them.

"What happened?" she asked.

"It was a car accident," her dad said.

She turned, surprised. "A car accident? Was he doing some exotic car racing adventure or something?"

Her dad shook his head solemnly. "Nothing like that. He and his girlfriend were driving home from dinner at her parents' house. They live here. A car ran a red light and plowed into them. The other driver took off."

Cindy was stunned. All the crazy stuff her brother had pulled over the years. All the needless risks. And here he was fighting for his life because of a hit-and-run driver. It seemed absurd.

"His girlfriend, is it Lisa?" she asked. It was still hard to say that name. She was glad her brother had found someone to care about, though, even if she did share the same first name as their dead sister.

"Yes, Lisa," her dad said. From the sound of his voice when he said her name she could tell he was having a hard time with it, too.

"Where is she?"

"She's in a different room. She's pretty banged up, too, but she was riding in the passenger seat and the car...the car was hit on the driver's side. The doctors think she'll be okay."

"Are her parents here?" Cindy asked.

"Yes. They're the ones who called us actually. They're...nice."

"Nice?" Cindy asked, noticing her father's hesitation.

"Yes. Odd, but nice."

She wanted to ask in what way they were odd. Actually she wanted to talk about anything other than her brother there on the other side of the glass fighting for his life.

Her dad looked at her. "You haven't met Lisa yet, have you?"

"No," Cindy admitted. "Kyle told me a little about her. He said she was an interior designer, that she was a genius."

"He's right about that. Lots of important people hire her. She's very sweet, though. She redid our entire living room and dining room area a few months ago. Wouldn't take a cent for it either."

Cindy nodded and turned back to the glass. She should go say hello to Lisa, meet her. She didn't feel up to it at the moment, though. She said a quick prayer for strength and that Kyle would recover so he could be the one to introduce them.

Her phone buzzed, and she pulled it out of her purse. Jeremiah had texted her.

Did you make it safe?

Yes. At hospital, she texted back. After a moment she added, *Will call later.*

Okay.

She put her phone away, and looked at her parents. How long had they been standing in front of the glass? Being in the observation room for just five minutes was terrifying her. What was it doing to them? There was nothing any of them could do but watch and wait and send dozens of whispered prayers heavenward.

A half hour dragged by and there was no change. She felt completely helpless in a way she hadn't in a long time. She was beginning to realize that she was hungry as well. The lunch she and Jeremiah hadn't managed to have was hours and hours ago. She pressed a hand over her stomach as it growled.

"I need to get something to eat," she finally said quietly so as not to startle her parents again.

Her dad stirred and turned to look at her. "There should be a cafeteria around here somewhere. I'll go with you."

"Okay. Mom?"

"I'm not hungry," her mother said without turning away from the glass.

"We'll bring her something to eat," her father said.

Fifteen minutes later the two of them were sitting down at a table in an isolated corner of the cafeteria. Even though she was starving, the meatloaf on Cindy's plate looked a lot less appetizing than it had sounded. She made a face as she dunked a bite in ketchup.

Across from Cindy her father picked up his hamburger and began eating. From the way he was doing it, she doubted he was even tasting the food, but rather just going through the motions of eating. Her own nerves were strained to the breaking point, and she couldn't even begin to imagine what he was feeling.

Her dad's eyes shifted to her as he swallowed the bite he'd been chewing. "How are things with the rabbi?" he asked.

"Okay," Cindy said, wondering why he was asking.

"Kyle told us he was an interesting fellow. Intense."

"He certainly is intense," Cindy said with a sigh.

"This is your first real long-term boyfriend, isn't it?"

The question caught her completely off-guard. "He's not my boyfriend," she finally managed to sputter.

Her father frowned. "I thought Kyle said he was."

Cindy rolled her eyes. "Kyle's been trying to get us together since he met Jeremiah a few months ago."

"Odd. That's not the impression he gave. Just as well, I guess, your mother wasn't too keen on the idea."

"What's wrong with... you know what, never mind," Cindy said.

She was suddenly very relieved that she had told Jeremiah not to come. This much awkward neither of them needed.

Her father continued eating his hamburger, and she managed to choke down some of the meatloaf. Cindy was struggling with what to say to him.

His phone rang and he snatched it off the table and brought it to his ear. "Hello? Yes. I'll be right there."

He stood up as he disconnected the call. "They're taking Kyle in for another round of surgery. The bleeding's gotten worse," he said.

Cindy started to stand up and he put a hand on her shoulder. "You need to eat, keep your strength up. There's nothing you can do right now."

"Mom-"

"I'll take care of her," he said.

Cindy swallowed hard. "Isn't there something I can do?"

He nodded. "Actually, I would appreciate it if you'd let Lisa know."

"Okay," Cindy said.

"She's in room 214. Finish your dinner first."

Cindy watched her father hurry from the room. She shoved the rest of her food in her mouth. She hadn't wanted to meet Lisa yet, but her father was right, she needed to know what was happening.

Finished, Cindy tossed her trash and then hurried to the elevator. A minute later she was walking timidly into room 214.

Her heart was in her throat. She didn't know what to expect. She wasn't sure how badly Lisa was injured or what the other woman would know about Kyle's condition or about Cindy. There were just too many unknowns and it was only adding to her anxiety.

Lisa was on the hospital bed, partially sitting up. Her red hair was pulled back from a pale face. There was bruising on her face and her right wrist was in a cast. She was talking to two people who were already in the room. Two things struck Cindy nearly simultaneously. Lisa was talking to two police officers and on Lisa's left hand there was an engagement ring.

Cindy stared in shock. Lisa wasn't just her brother's girlfriend. From the looks of the ring on her finger she was his fiancée. She wondered when that had happened. It had to be recent. Otherwise surely Kyle or their mother would have called. That wasn't the kind of news Cindy's mom could keep for half a second.

"You two got engaged?" she blurt out. Horrified, she looked up and met Lisa's tear-filled eyes.

"Last night," Lisa confirmed in a whispery voice.

"I'm sorry, miss? You can't be in here," one of the officers, a tall man with graying hair said.

"It's okay," Lisa said. "She's Kyle's sister."

Cindy's astonishment must have shown on her face, because Lisa went on to tell her, "I recognized you from the pictures I've seen."

Cindy nodded mutely as her brain seemed to switch gears. Now that the shock of the engagement ring was wearing off she wondered what the two police officers were doing there.

"You don't remember anything else about the car that hit you?" the other officer asked.

"No, it was dark and it came out of nowhere. By the time the car stopped spinning and sliding I didn't see it anywhere."

The tall one muttered something that sounded like "hate drunk tourists," under his breath.

Cindy cleared her throat. "I'm very sorry to interrupt and also very sorry to meet you under these circumstances, but my dad wanted me to tell you that Kyle's going in for another round of surgery. Apparently he's still bleeding a lot internally."

She was shocked that she managed to get through saying that without choking up. On some level she realized that all of this just wasn't real for her yet. The whole day had been one long, surreal nightmare it seemed.

Lisa nodded, biting her lip.

Having delivered her message, Cindy suddenly felt very weak and exhausted. It was as though everything that had happened that day caught up to her all at once. Given that she still hadn't had time to rest and recover after the chaos of Geanie and Joseph's wedding, it was probably amazing that she was still standing upright let alone speaking coherently.

"I guess I should go," she said uncertainly.

"No, stay, please," Lisa said, her eyes entreating.

Cindy nodded as she realized that she really had nowhere else to be at the moment. Kyle was in surgery, and her father would have his hands full with her mom. It was either sit and wait in a room pretty much by herself or sit and wait here with the woman her brother loved enough to marry.

There was a chair near the bed and Cindy sat down in it and leaned back slightly. She was exhausted, and she would give anything to just go get a hotel room and get some sleep. She knew she wouldn't be able to sleep, though. At least not until Kyle was out of surgery.

Lisa turned to the officers. "Are there any other questions?" she asked.

"Not at this time," the taller one said. "We will be in touch, though, and if you think of anything you have our card."

She nodded and the two officers left.

Lisa turned and gave Cindy a weak smile. "Not exactly how I pictured our first meeting," she said.

"Me either. Although it is good to finally meet you. Kyle told me a lot about you."

"And he talks about you constantly."

"He does?" Cindy asked, trying to mask her surprise.

"Yes. He's very proud of all the cases you help the police solve. It's like you're a real life Nancy Drew, only cooler."

Cindy felt her cheeks grow warm at the compliment. "And I hear you're a genius with interior design."

"Did you like what I did with your parents' place?"

Cindy sighed. "I haven't seen it, to be honest."

Lisa nodded. "That's right. I forgot that you don't ever go home."

Cindy winced. Hearing a stranger say it that way made it sound bad. There were lots of reasons she didn't, but none of them that she wanted to get into right now. "So, your parents live here in town?" she asked, trying to deflect.

"Just outside of town. I sent them home to get some rest just a little bit ago."

"I'm sure they needed it," Cindy said. She covered a yawn with her hand, and looked closely at Lisa. Aside from the bruises on her face her skin was bone white and there were dark circles under her eyes. "You could probably use some rest, too," she added.

Lisa shook her head. "I can't rest until I know Kyle is going to be okay."

"I'm sure he will be," Cindy said, lying for both their sakes.

Lisa's eyes shimmered with tears. "I just keep going over it and over it in my mind, thinking about what I could have done, how I could have stopped it from happening."

"My dad told me that you guys were hit when a car ran a red light," Cindy said. "There's nothing you can do about that. It was an accident."

"I know, but I keep thinking about...everything, you know?" Lisa said. "If we had hit that intersection one second sooner or one second later, then we would have spent the day celebrating our engagement. Instead we're here."

"You can't think like that," Cindy said, her heart breaking for the other woman. "Counting the seconds won't help you. I mean, maybe if you'd been a few seconds earlier or later you might have been in an even worse accident."

"I don't know how it could have been worse," Lisa sniffled as tears started to stream down her face.

You could have both been killed on impact, Cindy thought but decided not to say it out loud.

Instead she reached out and grabbed Lisa's good hand, and gave it a little squeeze. "So, tell me how Kyle proposed," she said.

Lisa smiled a little. "Kyle decided about a month ago that he wanted to meet my parents and so he arranged for us to take a quick vacation out here. When I visit I usually just stay with them. I tend to avoid the Vegas strip like the plague. Kyle made all the arrangements, though. I could tell he was going for a romantic gesture and he wouldn't be talked out of it. So, after a while, I gave up and just went with it."

"Sometimes with Kyle that's all you can do."

"I know, right? When he gets something in his head, he just has to see it through," Lisa said. "Half the time it's really charming and the other half it's..."

"Irritating?" Cindy suggested.

"Yes, exactly! Anyway, we checked into our hotel two days ago. He had booked us two rooms at the Excalibur. It's the one that's shaped like a castle. Anyway, he said he had some work calls to make but he told me he'd meet me in a couple of hours for dinner. Then he called and apologized. He said he was going to be running late, but that he didn't want me to miss anything. He'd gotten us tickets to the medieval dinner show at the hotel with all the knights on horseback jousting. He said he'd be there just as soon as he could."

Lisa paused and cleared her throat. Cindy quickly handed her a cup of water from the bedside tray, and Lisa drank it.

"Thank you," she said, handing the cup back.

"No problem. What happened next?"

"I went to the box office and picked up my ticket. We had seats in the first row of one of the sections. The knights came out on horseback, and they all looked magnificent. The master of ceremonies made an announcement and said that one knight was on a special crusade of his own that night. I kept looking for Kyle, sad that he was missing out. All of a sudden this one knight rode his horse right up to the edge of the arena until he was right in front of me. He tilted his lance forward and I noticed that there was a satin bow tied on it, and on the bow was a ring. He took off his helmet and it was Kyle."

Lisa's eyes were tearing up again. Cindy's were, too, as she pictured the scene playing out.

"He said that he would slay dragons for me, that he loved me. He asked me to marry him. I said 'yes' and untied the ring. A squire came and took his horse and he came to sit beside me. Everyone toasted us and cheered. It was amazing, crazy, so very, very over-the-top."

"So very Kyle," Cindy said with a choked laugh that ended as a sob.

Lisa nodded. "I barely even saw the rest of the show, I was so dazed. It turns out he knew some of the guys from one of his filming trips here and I guess he'd been planning this for a while."

"I know when I saw him back in November he seemed pretty sure you were the one," Cindy said, hoping it would bring Lisa comfort in some small way.

A nurse bustled in, interrupting, and Cindy took a moment to dry her eyes.

"You need to rest now," the nurse told Lisa, giving a significant glance at Cindy.

"I can't," Lisa protested.

"You must. I'm giving you something to help with that," the nurse said.

Cindy took the hint and stood shakily to her feet. "I'll see you in the morning," she promised Lisa who just nodded.

Out in the hall Cindy checked her phone. No messages from her father yet. She wanted to call Jeremiah, but she knew she'd completely lose it and she didn't want to sob uncontrollably in the hospital corridor. She leaned for a second against the wall, exhausted, spent, and unsure what to do with herself.

"Cindy? Are you okay?"

She glanced up at the sound of her name and stared at a man standing a couple of feet from her. It took her a moment, but she finally recognized him as Martin, the man who'd been next to her on the plane.

"I have to admit I kind of wondered if I'd run into you," he said.

She stared at him. "What are you doing here?"

"My job. I'm a salesman, remember? I sell hospital supplies and equipment. I was supposed to take the administrator of this hospital out to dinner tonight, but he had a family thing he had to deal with."

"Oh."

He took a step closer, his brow furrowing. "Seriously, are you okay? How's your brother?"

"Not good," she admitted.

"I'm sorry to hear that. Is he in there?" he said, gesturing to the room she'd just left.

"No, his fiancée is in there. She's doing better than he is."

"Oh. Well, where are you headed?"

"I don't know," she said. It was the truth.

"Well, I haven't eaten, so care to join me downstairs? The cafeteria here isn't half bad."

"I've already eaten."

"Okay, then watch me eat and have a cup of coffee. You look like you need some caffeine to keep you going."

She had nowhere else to go and he was right, caffeine would probably be a good idea.

"Okay," she said with a weary nod. She took one step away from the wall and then stopped.

She was tired and not thinking quite straight, but she had a sudden pressing question she needed him to answer. "You're not going to like try to kill me or kidnap me or anything, are you?"

It sounded absurd even as she was saying it.

"Excuse me?" he asked, eyebrows raising incredulously. "Ah, no. Do I look like a killer or a kidnapper?"

"No, but you'd be surprised how many people are and don't look like it."

He took a step backward, hands partially raised.

"I'm sorry," she said. "I'm really tired and I've been through some...stuff...the last few years."

"Clearly," he said, nodding. He still looked wary, though.

"You're right. I need some caffeine. Shall we go?"

He lowered his hands. "Okay. Hey, at least since we're in a public place we know we're both safe."

If only it was that simple, she thought. Fortunately she kept herself from voicing it out loud. Martin would probably run screaming at that point, and really, who would blame him?

Five minutes later, for the second time that night she found herself sitting down at a table in the cafeteria. Normally she was a soda drinker, but she had opted instead for strong, black tea. She cradled the warm cup in her hands and savored the sensation. She had placed her phone on the table so she could stare at it from time-to-time willing it to ring.

Martin had opted for a meal that looked like pot roast and mashed potatoes and he was digging into it with abandon. "I love good food," he said, after his fifth forkful.

"And that counts?" she asked.

"Most certainly. It's recognizable and it's comfort food. You wouldn't believe some of the places I've been and what I've eaten there."

She sipped her tea while he continued to eat. Finally he began to slow down. "You know, you really need to get some rest. You look like you're about to drop," he said, before gulping some coffee.

"I can't. Not until my brother Kyle gets out of surgery at least," she said.

He frowned. "You know, one of the doctors was telling me they had a famous Kyle in the hospital."

Cindy nodded gloomily. "That's my brother. Kyle Preston."

"That travel guy?"

"Yes. Let me guess, you're a fan?" Cindy asked. She drank some more tea, enjoying the warmth of it as it went down her throat.

"To be honest, I've only caught one or two shows, but I'm pretty sure my kid sister wants to bear his children."

Cindy spewed tea on the table. "Oh my gosh! I am so sorry," she said, hurriedly grabbing some of his napkins to mop it up.

"My fault. I think I made an inappropriate joke."

"No, it's just, I've never heard it put that way before," Cindy said, still embarrassed as she finished mopping up the liquid.

"Well then you don't know my sister. I believe that was one of her Facebook posts last month. She'll be devastated to hear that he has a fiancée."

She'll be even more devastated if he dies.

Cindy shook her head. She shouldn't think like that.

Her phone rattled to life on the table and she jumped. "Hello?" she asked breathlessly as she snatched it up.

It was her dad. He sounded tired. "He's out of surgery. We still don't know much of anything."

"Okay, where are you?"

"In the lobby at the moment. I booked us a room at the hotel across the street. I think we're going to head over in a few minutes. We're both exhausted. The nurses have reassured me they'll call if there's any change. You want to come with us?"

"Yes, I'll be there in a minute," Cindy said.

She ended the call. "He's out of surgery, and it sounds like my folks and I are all going to go get some sleep," she explained.

"Good, you need it," Martin said.

"I have to go, I'm sorry."

"No, go. You've got my card. If you need anything, just give me a call."

"Thanks," she said.

She scooped up her trash and tossed it on her way out of the room. She hurried upstairs and found her parents waiting for her. They headed outside, and she was surprised at just how bright it was for being nighttime. The sky was lit up by all the artificial lights of the city.

They went down to the corner and crossed the street. Her father was right, the hotel entrance was literally right there. They walked inside, encountering slot machines right next to the door. A few minutes later they were staggering into their room. It was cramped, but it had two queen beds. Cindy sat down wearily on the one by the window. She hadn't had to share a hotel room with her parents since she was in high school. Apparently, though, it was the only one available. It seemed there was a medical conference going on. She wondered if that's why Martin was here at this particular time.

Her parents had brought a suitcase that had stuff thrown haphazardly in it. She didn't have anything with her.

In her pocket she felt her phone vibrate and she pulled it out. Jeremiah had texted her.

How's it going?

She had promised she would call him. There was no way she was doing that in front of her parents, though. She forced herself to her feet. "I need to go down to the gift shop and grab some sundries," she said.

"You need money?" her dad asked as he stood, gazing at a mismatched pair of pajamas.

"No, I'm good."

Her mom was just sitting on the edge of the bed, staring into space.

Cindy made it out of the room and headed downstairs. She had seen a store in the lobby when they'd checked in. Hopefully she could get some necessities there. What she most wanted was a toothbrush and a pair of pajamas.

Fortunately, she found both. The pajamas had a playing card motif on them but looked comfortable. She went ahead and bought herself a deck of cards, too. She didn't have a deck in her purse currently and she needed something to fidget with.

Once she had purchased the items she walked out of the store. A minute later she found a chair by a hotel courtesy phone in a small alcove that was a little less noisy than the rest of the area. She sat down and pulled out her phone to call Jeremiah.

"Hello?"

She closed her eyes and felt herself relax slightly at the sound of his voice. Regardless of all the craziness they'd had that day just hearing his voice made her feel better, safer somehow.

"Hey, it's me," she said.

"How are you?"

"Better than I expected to be, honestly. Kyle just came out of another surgery for internal bleeding, and we don't know much else at this point. My parents are a wreck although Dad is holding it together better than Mom is. Kyle's fiancée is banged up and has a broken wrist but otherwise seems okay. She's nice.

"Fiancée?"

"Yeah, apparently they got engaged two days ago. Seems like everyone's getting married. Well, if he survives, he will be. It's just such a mess," she said.

She could hear the exhaustion in her own voice, and that was never a good thing.

"So, what happened?"

"It was an accident. They were driving back from her parents' house when some idiot ran a red light, slammed into their car, and then took off."

Jeremiah was silent for so long she finally asked, "Are you still there?"

"Yes, sorry. I was just thinking. Are you sure it was an accident?"

"That's what they're saying. Why?"

"It's just, the last time Kyle was the victim of accidents, it turned out not to be so...accidental."

She knew he was referencing the cattle drive that they had all been on together. "I hadn't thought about it," she said quietly. "He's here on vacation, though, so it can't be a work thing."

"Hasn't he done shows in Vegas before?"

"Yeah."

"Maybe someone he encountered back then has some kind of issue with him."

"I hope not," Cindy said, pressing her free hand to her forehead which was beginning to throb. She'd have to remember to go back into the store and grab some aspirin.

"Sorry, I'm still jumpy from last week. I'm sure I'm just being paranoid," Jeremiah said swiftly, as though sensing her distress.

"I know, I had a hard time believing with all the crazy risks he takes and stunts he pulls that this is all because of something so common as a car accident. It's just a crazy, unexpected accident."

Like our sister.

She bit her lip, focusing on the pain so she wouldn't start crying at the thought. She pulled it back together and then quickly asked, "How are things there?"

He paused for a moment and then said, "That guy Christopher showed up at my house asking for my help to prove that his boss is innocent before the man's reputation is irredeemably trashed."

"Wow. What did you say?"

"I said 'no'. I have too many other things going on, and I am not interested in getting that close to the situation given how many reporters are going to be covering every aspect of it."

"Kind of goes against that whole 'the man of mystery in the shadows' thing, doesn't it?"

He actually chuckled which made her smile. "A little bit."

"I really don't believe that guy did it."

"Well, when you get back I'm sure you can figure out who did."

"Yeah, but Christopher was right about one thing. Every hour that suspicion is on him makes it that much harder for him to recover politically even if he is exonerated. Besides, what if the real killer goes free? Then I'd end up having to testify at his trial as to what I saw and an innocent man could go to jail. I couldn't deal with that."

Jeremiah sighed on the other end of the line. "Cindy, do you want me to work on this and keep you in the loop?"

"Yes, please."

There wasn't anything she could do to help her brother, but there was something she could do to help Henry.

"Alright. I'll do it for you," he said.

"Thank you."

"Now go get some rest."

"I will," she promised.

"And call the minute you know anything."

"You, too."

"Goodnight," he said.

"Goodnight."

Reluctantly she ended the call. She sat there for a moment just taking in deep breaths. Aspirin. She remembered that she needed to go back into the store and get some.

She put her phone in her purse and then picked up her shopping bag. She stood and started crossing the lobby toward the store.

Out of the corner of her eye she saw something moving quickly. She turned her head just as something slammed into her. She staggered, nearly falling, and she felt her purse being ripped out of her hand.

She turned just in time to see a man in a hoodie sprinting toward the front doors of the hotel. He was carrying her purse.

"Stop, thief!" Cindy shrieked as loudly as she could.

A security guard rushed forward and the thief sidestepped him. The front of the hotel had a bank of doors and he was heading for the one on the right. Before he got there, one of the doors in the middle opened and Martin walked inside, a newspaper under one arm.

"Martin! Stop him!" Cindy shrieked, pointing frantically.

He turned, saw the thief just steps away, and dove at his legs, tackling him to the ground. Cindy's purse flew out of the man's hands and landed a couple of feet away.

The security guard rushed forward, put one knee on the thief's back, grabbed his arms and handcuffed them behind his back. Other people in the lobby burst into spontaneous applause.

Martin reached over and retrieved her purse.

"Don't move," she heard the guard tell the guy on the ground.

She raced up. "Thank you!"

"When I said to call me if you needed anything, this wasn't exactly what I had in mind," Martin panted as he straightened up and handed Cindy her purse.

"I'm sorry. Thank you. Wow. How did you learn to do that?"

"I played football in high school. Plus, I have three older brothers."

Cindy clutched her purse tightly. "Well, thank goodness for football and older brothers."

The police arrived in what seemed like record time. It turned out they had already been in the vicinity taking the statement of another purse snatching victim. Apparently she had not been as lucky as Cindy, though.

"Doesn't that seem a little coincidental?" she quietly asked Martin as the one officer hauled the thief to his feet.

The guard overheard. "It's the most common crime here in Vegas. Some thieves just lift your wallet, even right out of your purse and you might not know it for hours. It makes it hard to catch and prosecute some of these guys. I'd keep a good hold on yours from now on."

"Thank you, I will," she said. She didn't bother to point out that she'd had a good hold on it earlier, but it hadn't mattered because of the amount of force the thief had used.

"Ma'am, are you willing to press charges?" the officer who didn't have hold of the thief asked.

She nodded.

"We'd appreciate it if you could come down to the station with us and help fill out some papers."

Before she could say anything Martin intervened. "Could she come in tomorrow? Her brother is in critical condition in the hospital, and she's desperately in need of some sleep."

"That would be fine. I do need to get your contact information, though."

Cindy nodded, grateful to Martin for speaking up. She wasn't sure she could have handled dealing with anymore that night. She gave the officer her information and a brief explanation of what had happened. He gave her his card with the address for the station on it.

They took the criminal away and Cindy began to breathe easier.

"Can I walk you to your room?" Martin asked.

"Make sure I don't get into any more trouble?" she joked.

He nodded.

"No, thank you. But you can walk me to the elevator after I get something else from the store."

"Will do."

It took just a minute for Cindy to buy the aspirin. Then Martin dutifully walked her to the elevator. They both got on and she noticed that his floor seemed to be the one above hers.

"Thank you again," she said as she got off at her floor.

"You're welcome."

She made it back into the room and realized that her parents were both already in bed asleep. She quickly got ready for bed, turned off the lights, and slid underneath the covers. The moment she closed her eyes she, too, was asleep.

Jeremiah was on the computer looking up everything he could about Henry White. After half an hour he concluded that the man was either a sincere visionary or an incredibly skillful manipulator. The whole premise of the man's campaign was that California was in deep trouble and the problems that people had been skirting for years needed to be faced head-on if the state was going to recover and once again thrive. He further contended that no one could truly understand the problems of the people of the state without first having walked in their shoes.

White's subsequent walk across the state had garnered a ton of supporters and quite a few detractors who threw around the words "cheap stunt" as if by saying it often enough it would make it true.

He had to give the man credit, though. He truly was walking the length of the entire state. He wasn't even going in a perfectly straight line. There was some zigzagging so that he stepped foot in every county in the state. Most of his campaign team, including his wife, were driving between the speaking engagements and setting up before he got there and tearing down after he left. There were only a couple of staffers who were walking the entire way with him and they were documenting every mile with photos that had been blasted all over social media.

Some of his supporters were walking with him, too. Most of them were just walking a few miles or a few days. There were many who would walk with him across their own county, and some events had turned into half-parade half-political march.

The willingness to walk all those hundreds of miles took a dedication, focus and a purpose that seemed incompatible with the thought of him killing someone, particularly in so sloppy a way. A man like this was thoughtful, a planner who saw the big picture. Someone like that didn't throw months of work away. It didn't make sense.

Add to that Cindy's belief that the man was innocent and Jeremiah was starting to buy into that theory as well. Killing a girl in a woman's room at a campaign stop and getting caught was sloppy and just didn't fit with the picture he was beginning to get of the man.

As much as he didn't want to do it, he finally called Christopher.

"Hello?" the other man answered, tension in his voice.

"This is Jeremiah. You were at my house earlier."

"Yes, I know who you are."

No, you really don't, he thought to himself.

"Look, I believe that Henry White is innocent, and I'll try to help you prove that under one condition."

"Anything," Christopher said eagerly.

"My involvement remains our little secret. I don't want any dealings with the press."

"You have my word," Christopher said.

Jeremiah wasn't sure how much value to give that, but at least it was a start.

"Okay, I'll be in touch," he said before hanging up.

Next he called Liam. The detective sounded tired when he answered.

"Rough day?" Jeremiah asked sympathetically. He had a feeling it was Liam's first time working on a case that was getting what was likely national attention at this point.

"The worst."

"I'm about to make it either better or worse depending on your point of view."

"I can't wait," Liam said.

Jeremiah was pretty sure the man had been going for sarcastic, but instead he just sounded exhausted.

"Christopher has asked for me to help look into this whole mess. Both Cindy and I believe that Henry is innocent."

Liam sighed audibly. "Look, you can't get involved."

"We're already involved, remember? Besides, you'll be needing to talk things over with someone since Mark is out of town. That reminds me, Cindy had to leave as well. Her brother was in an accident so she's in Vegas at the moment."

"Great. She's a key witness."

"She got the call, and had to drop everything to go. I'll help you with whatever I can since she and I discussed things pretty thoroughly."

"I shouldn't say yes to you helping."

"But you're going to because Mark isn't here and you don't know who else you can safely talk to without worrying that your words are going to be leaked to the press."

"I'm not sure if I'm angrier at Mark for not being here or at you for knowing that's what I'm worried about."

"Be angrier at Mark. He's not here to defend himself. Besides, you and I have work to do."

"Okay," Liam agreed. "We'll blame Mark."

Mark woke slowly, feeling the sun warm on his face. When he finally opened his eyes he saw Traci standing at the window staring out at the ocean. She was wearing a white satin gown that clung to her in all the right places. She turned to look at him with a soft smile. Light haloed around her hair making her look like an angel.

That's what she was. She was his glorious, wonderful angel. Her smile widened and all the cares and heartache of the last year just seemed to slip away. He stood up and walked over to her. He wrapped his arms around her waist and she leaned back against his chest and together they stared out at the incredibly blue water.

"Did you sleep okay?" he asked.

"Yes. The bed was so soft. How did you sleep?"

"Sounder than I've slept in a long time. I'm on vacation."

He had to admit that when Joseph planned a dream vacation the man knew what he was doing. Their room was actually a grass hut on their own pier jutting out into the crystalline waters. The smell of the ocean air and the sound of the waves had lulled him to sleep the night before and it had been a deep, dreamless sleep that refreshed body and soul.

They stood that way for a few more minutes before Traci turned in his arms and kissed him. He smiled as she pulled away. "Are you ready for breakfast?"

"Lead the way," he told her.

Twenty minutes later they entered the resort's restaurant. They were in French Polynesia and the restaurant was very French. The maître d' had a French accent and quickly seated them at a table for two fronting the ocean.

They had gotten in late the night before and had both just had a light dinner. Meals were included in their trip package and it was a rare treat to be able to scan the menu and know he could order whatever he wanted without having to worry about the price.

"The crepes sound good," Traci said as she perused the menu.

"They do," he agreed, as he closed his. He remembered ice cream being on the dessert menu last night, and that had given him an idea.

A minute later their waiter had appeared to take their order.

"I'd like the strawberry banana crepes with a side of bacon," Traci said, surrendering her menu.

"Excellent, and for you, monsieur?"

"I'd like a banana split," Mark said.

Traci stared at him. "For breakfast?" she asked.

He shrugged. "I'm on vacation."

"Very good, sir," the waiter said with what Mark thought was an approving smile.

The banana split was magnificent and as he savored every bite he reflected that yes, this was what being on vacation should feel like and taste like. Traci kept laughing at him as he savored his meal with an assortment of happy sounds.

She was done eating before he was which was a first. Usually he was the one bolting down his food and barely tasting anything. He was going to have to thank Joseph for sending them somewhere that he could have a banana split for breakfast.

The waiter led a well-dressed woman past their table and Traci grabbed Mark's hand with a little gasp.

"What is it?" he asked.

"That woman, I know who she is!"

He glanced over just as the waiter was pulling out a chair for the woman in question. She had wavy, red hair and pale skin with a hint of a tan. She dressed well enough to be a celebrity, but it was no one he could remember having seen before.

"I don't recognize her."

"It's Elisa Roberts."

"Who?"

"She's a famous romance novelist. I've read most of her books. I recognized her from the picture on the back cover of the last one."

"Do you want to go get her autograph?"

Traci shook her head. "No, I'm sure she's here on vacation and just wants to be left alone."

"Do you want me to go get her autograph?" he asked.

"No! I'm good. Let's just let the woman eat in peace."

"Okay," he said, turning back to consume his last few spoonfuls of ice cream. He pushed the empty dish back at last with a contented sigh.

He pretended he didn't notice that Traci kept staring over at the writer. It was clear she did want an autograph; she was just too shy to ask for it. She didn't go into introvert mode often, but when she did it was always adorable somehow.

A couple of minutes later they left the restaurant and walked slowly back to their hut, fingers interlaced as they strolled. They began to walk down the long pier, and Traci leaned her head on his shoulder. "It's so beautiful. I wish we could stay here forever."

Once inside their hut Traci walked over to a table and began leafing through the brochures. "What do we want to do today? Go sailing, snorkeling, explore the island?"

"Actually I was thinking of grabbing a towel and having a nap on the beach," he admitted.

She raised an eyebrow. "A nap? You?"

He shrugged. "I'm on vacation."

She smiled at him. "So you are. You know what, I think a nap on the beach sounds wonderful. Is there room on that towel for two?"

"There's even room for three," he said, staring pointedly at her midsection.

She flushed and smiled. "I guess it is the three of us now."

"And I couldn't be happier about anything," he said.

Half an hour later they were wearing their bathing suits, had thoroughly applied sunscreen, and were laying out on the beach, soaking up the warmth. Mark had his eyes closed and he thought he might never open them again. There was only a handful of other people on the beach, but they were all so spread out it almost felt like they had their own private beach.

He was going to have to thank Joseph for sending them somewhere they could just completely relax and let go of all their cares.

Traci was reading a book, but he was just resting, letting go of all the stress and frustration of the last year. The whole mess with Paul, the weeks he had been suspended from the force, the stress of all the kidnappings, all of it. It was just as if it was all melting away beneath the tropical sun.

As the frustrations of the past left him he found himself daydreaming about the future. They didn't know yet whether they'd be having a girl or a boy, but either way was great with him. He couldn't wait to be a father and Traci was going to make a terrific mother.

When they got home there was so much to do to start preparing, but he vowed that from then on he would spend less time working and more time with his family. He smiled at the thought.

For the moment, though, his only responsibility was to relax and have fun with his wife. He couldn't think of anything better in the world. His mind began to drift and he was just about to fall asleep.

Suddenly the warm air was split by a high, piercing scream.

He sat upright, heart pounding.

A moment later he heard a woman shriek, "He's been murdered!"

The other people on the beach got up and ran toward the sound. Traci swiveled her head to look and see what was happening. He forced himself to sit very still.

A moment later Traci turned and looked at him, eyes full of concern. He just stayed put, forcing himself to breathe deeply.

"Aren't you going to go see what's going on?

He couldn't help but think that he was *not* going to be thanking Joseph for sending them somewhere that someone was murdered.

He shook his head. "I'm on vacation."

8

Mark was in turmoil. Every instinct he had was screaming at him to go and find out what was happening. Being a cop wasn't just a job, it was a lifestyle. You couldn't just leave that part of you at work every day. That was one of the number one stresses of the job and it could take a toll on a marriage. He was lucky that he had the most understanding wife in the world, but he never wanted to take advantage of that. Traci deserved a husband who was one hundred percent focused on her when they were together.

Besides, he was a tourist on vacation. This wasn't his jurisdiction. It wasn't even his country. If the positions were reversed the last thing he would want was an outsider meddling in his investigation no matter who they were. The best and smartest move was to let the locals handle it.

"There are so few residents on this island," Traci said softly. "Do you think the police have ever had to deal with a murder before?"

"I'm sure they have," he said, trying to reassure both of them. "And if not, they could always bring out someone from one of the other islands."

They weren't on the most populous island, Tahiti, but were on Bora Bora which he'd read about briefly on the plane. The island had one-tenth the number of residents as their hometown.

"I'm sure they don't need my help," he said.

Traci eyed him intently. "Because someone who's brought hundreds of murderers to justice has no skills that would be helpful in this situation."

"I'm on vacation," he reiterated.

"The Mark that I know wouldn't be able to stand being so close to a mystery and not trying to solve it," she said.

He sighed. Whenever Traci wanted to prove a point and appeal to his better nature she always played *The Mark that I Know* card. How did he tell her that all the unsolved craziness in his life, much of it revolving around Paul, had burnt him out? Looking deep into her eyes he knew it was something he couldn't tell her.

"Okay, I'll just go and see what happened," he said.

She gave him a dazzling smile as he stood up.

It wasn't difficult to figure out where all the commotion was since everyone who had been in the vicinity seemed to be flocking toward the nearest hut. People were crowded on the pier, craning their necks to see what was happening.

A hotel employee, whom Mark guessed to be a manager from the way he carried himself, was trying to push his way through the crowd. Mark followed in his wake. Just outside the hut's door, a bikini-clad woman in her early thirties was sobbing. She was probably the one who had screamed.

Next to her was the writer that Traci had been staring at during breakfast. She had her arm around the crying woman and was making soothing noises. Her eyes, though, were roving over the scene, clearly taking in every detail.

The manager moved past them to stand in the open doorway and look inside the hut. When he turned back a moment later he looked like he was going to be sick.

Mark stepped up to him. "I'm a homicide detective here on vacation. I'll help in whatever way I can."

"I've already called for the police," the man said, eyes dazed. "What should I do?"

"Get these people back off the pier before they contaminate the crime scene," Mark said.

The man nodded. "I can do that." He turned to the crowd and lifted his arms. "Ladies and gentlemen, I need you all to move back onto the beach right now."

"Is someone really dead?" a woman asked.

"What's going on?" a man chimed in.

"Please, we will know more later. For now, I need everyone to move before I have to call security to make you move. For your cooperation, mixed drinks at the Terrace will be free for the next half hour."

Mark had to hand it to the guy. He might be on the verge of losing his breakfast, but he knew how to disperse a crowd. They all turned and quickly headed for the bar and their free drinks.

"Nice work," Mark said quietly.

The manager shrugged. "You'd be surprised what people will do to get something for free."

"I'll have to remember that trick."

Mark turned and looked inside the hut. There, on the bed, was a man who looked to be in his late fifties. His face was bloated and blotchy looking. Mark scanned the area, looking for anything out of the ordinary. He didn't want to disturb any evidence that might be present.

He turned to the woman who was still crying in the writer's arms.

"Ma'am," he said, gently tapping her on the shoulder.

She straightened slowly, wiping at her eyes. "Yes?"

"Can you tell me what happened here?"

"My husband Milt and I came here to get away. He said it would be like a second honeymoon."

"How long have the two of you been married?"

"Six years," she said with a sniff.

There was probably a twenty-year age gap or more between husband and wife, Mark realized.

"He'd been real stressed out lately. Things had been rough at work. He started talking about people being out to get him. He even got a threatening letter at home one day, but he wouldn't talk to me about it," she said, dabbing at her eyes.

"Then he sprung this vacation on me. It was so spur-of-the-moment that it took my breath away. I didn't realize at that point that he was just trying to get away from...from...all the trouble."

"And what happened today?"

"After brunch we came back to the room. I wanted to go for a swim and he wanted to take a nap. He works such long, terrible hours that just napping is his favorite thing to do on vacation," she said with a sniffle. "I got changed and he was on the bed when I left. Then...when I came back...I found...found him...like that!" she ended with a wail.

"What did your husband do for a living?"

"He worked on Wall Street, financial investments."

"Did he say who "they" were, the ones out to get him?"

She shook her head. "No. I knew there was trouble at work, but he'd never say who or what. He'd just tell me not to worry my pretty little head about it."

He turned to the manager whose eyes were wide and panic-filled. "Nobody could have been poisoned at my resort," he said.

Mark held up a hand to calm the man down. "We don't know anything yet, and won't until your police have done a toxin screen. For all we know he died of a heart attack and that was all there was to it."

"This is a disaster," the other man muttered. "If word gets out about this..."

"Listen to me and focus. There's no need to spread panic and misinformation. All we know at the moment is that a man has died. How and why will be figured out later. Now, how long before the police arrive?"

"They should be here shortly."

"Good. Let me know when they get here. For now, let's get her someplace else where we can hopefully calm her down a bit."

"There's a couch in my office. She can lay down on that," he said.

"Perfect. Take her there, then come back."

"I'll go with her," the writer volunteered. "I'll talk to her, try to make more sense of things."

"Thank you, I would appreciate that."

She nodded.

"Follow me, ladies," the manager said, turning and heading toward the resort lobby. They followed, the widow leaning heavily on the romance novelist. Mark shook his head. There was irony there somewhere.

Now all he had to do was keep everyone out of the hut and wait for the police to show up and take charge of the scene. This was so not the way he had intended to spend his relaxing getaway with Traci.

Jeremiah had given up on sleep around three a.m. and had been back on the computer searching for more information about Henry White and the dead girl, Lydia Jenkins. When he found Lydia's Facebook page, the first thing that jumped out at him was that she didn't care about privacy, either hers or other people's. The second thing that struck him was that she had been a fan of Henry's. As he began scrolling through page after page of pictures he amended that. She wasn't just a fan. She appeared to be a full-fledged stalker. She had gathered an impressive number of pictures of him, both official press release photos and some incredibly candid ones that looked like they had been taken with him unaware that he was being photographed.

He wondered if the politician had known that Lydia was stalking him. He would have to ask Liam if the man had taken out any restraining orders against her. He found one album of photographs that was entirely dedicated to his walk across California campaign. There were pictures of her posing with Henry White in a dozen different locations.

So, she had been stalking him on the campaign trail. He wondered how many of the stops she had been there for.

He was just about to close the browser when one last picture caught his eye. It was of Lydia proudly showing off a Vote Henry White for California bumper sticker. It was on what looked like a green Honda. He was fairly certain he had seen that car in the First Shepherd parking lot the evening before. It had to be Lydia's. He wondered if the police had searched it yet.

He glanced at the clock. It was too early to call Liam. He was sure the detective would not thank him for rousing him out of sleep.

Jeremiah quickly got dressed and drove over to the church. Out of force of habit he parked at the synagogue. A minute later he was crossing through one of the paths in the hedge that separated the two lots. He was right. There was a green Honda sitting in the back third of the lot.

He approached it cautiously, walking slowly around it. There, on the back bumper, was the tell-tale political sticker from the picture. He was itching to get inside the car and see what he could find. He had gloves in the pocket of his jacket, and he could break in without leaving so much as a fingerprint.

If the car held real evidence, though, it was better to do this right. He pulled his phone out. Liam would just have to cope with the early wake-up call.

"Hello?" the detective said, clearly half-asleep.

"Hi, it's Jeremiah. Did you guys search Lydia's car yesterday at the church?"

"What? No. Is her car there?"

"Yeah, it is. I think you better come down here so we can open it and see what might be inside before someone else gets curious and comes to look."

"I'll be right there."

Twenty minutes later Liam pulled into the parking lot. He got out of his car, a coffee mug in one hand. He looked alert enough but the fact that his shirt was misbuttoned said otherwise. Jeremiah decided to point it out later.

"So, you're sure this is her car?" Liam asked.

Jeremiah nodded. "There was a picture of her showing off the bumper sticker on her Facebook page."

Liam nodded and took a sip of his coffee.

"So, what have you found out about Lydia?" Jeremiah asked.

"She was a grad student, getting a Masters in Political Science up at Sacramento State. Which explains how she came to be interested in Henry White."

"Obsessed with him is more like it," Jeremiah said. "There were hundreds of pictures of him on her Facebook page. A lot were quite intimate and he didn't appear to know he was being photographed."

"A stalker, huh? Her roommate said that she was following the campaign very closely and that she had gone to a lot of the rallies. I guess she didn't know just how deep the obsession ran."

"Or she was trying not to say anything negative about her," Jeremiah said.

"When I talked to the roommate last night she said Lydia was pretty upset Saturday morning when she showed up to grab some clean clothes and then left, presumably to drive down here. She just kept muttering 'not right' and 'needs to know'."

"She didn't happen to say what wasn't right or who needed to know, did she?"

"Unfortunately no."

"Well, let's take a look inside her car," Jeremiah suggested. "Maybe there's a clue in there as to what she was talking about or who killed her or why."

"Not so fast. I've got one of the crime scene guys coming to go over it."

Jeremiah was frustrated and feeling impatient. He should have just checked out the car himself before calling Liam.

Fortunately a car pulled into the parking lot five minutes later with the techs who proceeded to unlock the

Honda and go over every square inch of it. Jeremiah and Liam watched the progress silently.

When at last they had finished Jeremiah turned to Liam. "You know what they didn't find?"

"What?"

"A cell phone or a camera."

"Neither of those were at the crime scene," Liam said.

"Strange, don't you think?"

"I guess. Why?"

"Lydia took hundreds of pictures of White and about a dozen with him. In fact, everywhere the man went she seemed to have some sort of camera trained on him. So, what happened to it?"

"That's a very good question."

Jeremiah nodded. "I'm guessing if you find her camera, you'll find your killer."

"The question is why take the camera or the phone or whatever it was?"

"I'd be willing to bet Lydia took a picture someone never wanted the world to see, and that picture is what got her killed."

Cindy woke up feeling almost worse than she had the night before. She hadn't slept well; her dreams had been plagued by dark, shadowy figures that seemed to mock her at every turn. She sat up slowly and looked around. Her parents had already left. Pajamas had been flung on the other bed haphazardly. She wondered how long ago her parents had gotten up as she forced herself out of bed.

If they'd had word about Kyle they surely would have woken her up. She checked her phone. No messages. That was a good sign. She made it into the bathroom and took a quick shower, hoping the hot water would wake her up. Instead she caught herself nodding off. She forced her eyes back open. She had a difficult day ahead of her and she couldn't start it off by falling asleep in the shower and hurting herself.

Once dressed she called her dad's phone.

He picked up right away. From the sound of his voice she could tell that he hadn't slept well either.

"Is there any change?" she asked.

"No."

"Okay. I have to take care of a couple of things and then I'll come over later this morning."

"I'll call if anything changes," he promised.

"Thanks. Do you need anything?"

"No."

She finished getting ready, grateful that he hadn't asked her what things she needed to take care of. The last thing either of her parents needed to deal with right now was the fact that she'd had her purse snatched. It was the last thing she wanted to be dealing with, too, but what could she do? If she didn't make a statement the police would have a more difficult time trying to send the man to jail. If he went free then he'd be back on the streets robbing someone else.

She headed downstairs, and made her way to the hotel restaurant to get some breakfast. As she followed the hostess through a maze of tables she spotted a familiar figure seated by himself.

"Martin!" she called.

The man jerked and turned around in his chair, eyes sweeping the room. She gave a little wave and he nodded then smiled. He touched his ear briefly, and then he waved to an empty chair. "Care to join me?"

"Sure."

The hostess turned and went to Martin's table. She put the menu down for Cindy, and then headed back to the front of the restaurant. Cindy slid into the chair across from Martin's.

"I didn't mean to startle you," she said as she picked up her menu.

"It's okay. I'm afraid I'm not much of a morning person."

"I understand."

"How's your brother?"

"No change, I'm afraid."

"Well, if I've learned one thing over the years it's that where there's life, there's hope."

She nodded, and then perused her menu. She was so tired and stressed, though, that all the words just seemed to jumble together and the few she did manage to read she had to re-read twice before they would stick in her brain.

"May I make a suggestion?" Martin asked after a minute.

"Please do," she said with a frustrated sigh as she set the menu down.

"French toast. I just had some, and it was excellent."

"That sounds like a winner to me."

After the waiter came and took her order she slumped slightly in her chair. She really was exhausted.

Martin frowned at her. "You look like you should try to go get some more sleep."

She shook her head. "I've got to go down to the police station. Then it's back to the hospital."

"As long as you make it to the police station sometime today I'm sure you'll be fine. And your folks will call if there's any change at the hospital. You do have your phone on you, don't you?"

"Yes," Cindy said, reaching into her bag to check and see if there were any messages on it. She felt around for her phone for a minute and then realized she'd left it on the nightstand up in the room.

"Dang it."

"What's wrong?"

"I must have left my phone up in the room. I'm glad I checked. Now I'll have to go all the way back upstairs to get it before I head to the police station."

"You've got time to go grab it now before your food shows. That way you'll be free to head out as soon as you're finished."

"I guess I do. I'll be right back."

He nodded as he picked up his coffee mug and took a sip.

Fortunately it didn't take her long to make it back to the room, grab her phone, and get back downstairs. A minute after she sat down the waiter brought her food.

After a couple of bites she admitted, "You're right, it is good." She was surprised she could even taste anything with the state she was in. As it was she wolfed down all the food in what had to be record time.

He smiled at her when she had finished. "Feel a bit more ready to deal with the day?"

"Yes, actually."

"It's surprising how much a good meal can brighten your mood and give you energy."

"You're right."

"Well, good luck with your day. I'm sure I'll bump into you later. Now, though, I have to get to a meeting," he said, rising. "And don't worry about the check, I already took care of it."

She stared at him in shock. "You didn't need to do that."

He shrugged. "It's a small thing, but it was what I could do for you."

"Thank you. I really appreciate it."

"Do me a favor and just try to take it easy today."

She gave him a smile.

Martin left the restaurant, and a minute later she followed suit. Outside the lobby the doorman was able to hail a cab for her and moments later she was on her way to the police station. At the front desk she explained who she was and why she was there. An officer escorted her to a small room to wait for someone to come and take her statement.

She sat alone for almost half an hour, compulsively checking her phone for messages every couple of minutes. She had taken the deck of cards she'd bought the night before out of her purse and kept cutting them one-handed, grateful that she had something to fidget with. Finally an officer came in. She recognized him as one of the ones who had been talking to Lisa in her hospital room.

"Sorry to keep you waiting so long, Miss Preston," he said.

"It's okay. Did you find the driver that hit Kyle and Lisa?"

He hesitated slightly before saying, "We don't have any new information to share on that."

She quickly picked up on the words "to share". That didn't mean they didn't know anything new, it just meant they weren't willing to talk about it. She pressed a little harder. "I'm heading to the hospital as soon as I'm done here and I know everyone's looking for some glimmer of hope that you'll catch the guy."

"I understand, ma'am, but there's nothing I can say at this time."

"Okay," she said, frustrated because she knew he was holding out on her.

He sat down across the table from her and cleared his throat. "Now, as I understand it, you told the clerk at the desk that you're here on a different matter. A purse snatching, is that correct?"

"Yes. I agreed to come down here this morning and give my full statement so charges could be pressed."

"And who did you agree to this with?"

"The two officers who arrested the thief," Cindy said.

"So, let me make sure I've got this straight. Your purse was snatched last night by a thief. He was stopped, and two officers came and arrested him and told you to come down here today?"

"Well, there's a few more points and complications to the story, but yes, that's basically what happened."

"I see. Did you happen to get the name of the arresting officers?"

"No, but one of them gave me this card," she said, pulling it out of her purse and handing it to him.

He took it and stared at it with a frown. "It's just a standard card with the address," he said.

Alarm bells started going off in her head. "Is there something wrong?" she asked.

He set the card down on the table and finally met her eyes. "I'm not sure what to say. The truth is, we have no record of a purse snatching incident last night involving you or the hotel you're staying at."

"You're joking," she said, feeling a twisting sensation in her stomach.

"Trust me, ma'am, I wish I was."

"How is that possible? Two officers came and arrested him. They wanted me to come in last night for a statement, but Martin told them how tired I was, and they said I could come in this morning. Then they took him away."

"Who is Martin?"

"He's the man who tackled the guy after he stole my purse."

"Did he call the police?"

"No, the security guard at the hotel did. The officers showed up really quickly and they said they'd just finished investigating another purse snatching in the area."

"Ma'am, could you describe the officers?" he asked.

"They both had brown hair and were of medium height. I think I would recognize them if I saw them again."

"What about the purse snatcher?"

She shook her head. "He was wearing a hoodie and I never really got a look at his face."

The officer leaned back in his chair, his brow furrowing. "How about the security guard?"

"He was older, in his fifties, with white hair. He was kind of short."

"And his ethnicity?"

"He was Caucasian."

The officer was silent for a long minute. Finally he cleared his throat. "Ma'am, can you tell me what medications you routinely take?"

"What? Nothing, why?" she asked, startled.

"With everything that's happened to your brother I realize that you're under a great deal of strain."

"What does that have to do with anything? What is going on?" she demanded. She could feel her heart begin to pound. Something was very, very wrong here.

"Sometimes when a person is under a lot of stress they can have problems dealing with what's going on," he said slowly.

"I don't understand any of this."

"It's possible that you had a dream or perhaps an hallucination-"

She shoved back her chair and stood to her feet, anger flaring through her. "I'm not crazy! Dozens of people in that lobby saw what happened. They applauded when Martin tackled the thief to the ground. I don't know what's going on here, but two of your police officers came and took the man away. I'm here to give my statement about the whole incident. Now, would you like to help me figure out what's going on here?"

He stared up at her, eyes veiled, and she decided that this had to be what going crazy felt like, when you knew something and yet noone else believed you.

There was a sudden knock on the door. The officer went over and opened it. "I'll take over from here," a female voice said.

He nodded and left. A woman a couple of years older than Cindy came in and sat down across from her. She had short brown hair and matching brown eyes. She was wearing a navy pantsuit and she looked like the type of person who didn't pull their punches. As soon as the door had shut behind the other officer she leaned forward, eyes squinting intently.

"So, are you crazy or an attention junkie?" she asked.

"Excuse me?" Cindy said. "I'm neither, but something is very wrong around here."

"You know what happened to the boy who cried wolf? He got eaten."

"I'm not making this up!" Cindy shouted, fury welling up within her. "I have far better things to do and more important places to be."

The woman nodded and sat up straight. "I believe you. Now have a seat."

Reluctantly Cindy sat back down.

"I am Detective Sanders."

"Cindy Preston."

"Now, tell me everything that happened last night from the beginning."

Cindy recounted the events with as much detail as she could manage. The detective listened intently, asking the occasional question. When Cindy had finished the woman nodded.

"That's quite a story. Maybe we can sit you down with a sketch artist and work up some drawings of the guys involved."

"Okay. I can do that. But first it's your turn to answer some of my questions."

"Like what?" the detective asked, raising an eyebrow.

"If everyone thinks I'm crazy and there's no record of a purse snatching at my hotel last night, why is a detective talking with me? Don't you save this kind of attention for things like murder?"

"Or attempted murder, yes."

"That's what I thought. So, why are you talking to me? Nobody tried to kill me last night. A guy just stole my purse. I even got it back."

"Because I'm curious as to how your situation might link up with one of my investigations."

"I don't understand," Cindy said.

"Of course you don't. That's because you don't have the pertinent information."

"And that would be what?" Cindy asked.

"Your brother's accident."

"What about it?"

"It was no accident."

10

"Why are people always trying to kill Kyle?" Cindy burst out. She felt sick to her stomach at the revelation.

The detective looked at her sharply. "What do you mean?"

"Nothing," Cindy said, suddenly flustered.

"If you have information you're withholding that could help us get to the bottom of this that's not only illegal it's also a really bad idea."

"I'm not withholding anything related to this. A few months ago this crazy woman went after him during the filming of his new show. She thought if something happened to him then her boyfriend would get to host instead. Anyway, we caught her, and she's going to be in prison a very long time."

"Who's 'we'?"

"My friend Jeremiah, a detective from back home, and me."

"I think you better tell me about this," the detective said.

"It's in the past. It's not relevant."

"I'll be the judge of that."

Cindy took a deep breath and then summed up the events of the cattle drive for the other woman.

At the end of the story the detective shook her head. "Trouble does seem to have a way of finding him. I'll make a couple of phone calls and make sure that there haven't been any developments in that case that could shed light on this one, but I'm inclined to agree with you that they are unconnected. It's my understanding that this is not your brother's first trip to Vegas?"

"He's been here at least a couple of times filming."

"Can you be more specific?"

Cindy shook her head. "You'd have to ask my mother that one. She keeps much more up on his career than I do."

"From what I've heard, I'm not sure your mother is up to talking at the moment."

"That's true. She's pretty out of it. My dad or Lisa might be able to help with the same information."

"Alright, I'll follow up on that."

It was Cindy's turn to get some answers. "How do you know that it wasn't an accident?"

"A security camera on a building close to the intersection. We were able to see on the footage that the black sedan that hit your brother's car had been sitting about a hundred feet back from the intersection with its hazards on for two minutes, forcing other cars to go around. Then, the moment your brother started to enter the intersection, the guy hit the gas, and aimed straight at him. The car kept going after the impact, no hesitation or disoriented driving. That driver knew he was going to hit the other car and was prepared for it. Moreover, he was waiting for the opportunity to do so."

Cindy's mouth felt dry. "Could it have been a random act of violence or a case of mistaken identity?"

"I doubt it. So, what would be helpful is if you could tell me who might want to hurt your brother."

Cindy shook her head. "Lisa would probably know the answer to that better than I would. Kyle and I aren't exactly close."

"And yet you dropped everything to be here."

"Just because we don't see eye-to-eye on a lot of things doesn't mean I don't love him," Cindy said, feeling the heat rise in her cheeks. "And none of this explains why you think what happened to me last night is connected."

"I don't know if it is yet. It's just very suspicious. Someone nearly kills your brother and the very next night after you visited him in the hospital someone tries to steal your purse in what was clearly not a simple act of theft."

"How do you know that it wasn't?"

"Because whoever orchestrated that little theft had fake cops come to arrest the man who did it called by a fake hotel security guard."

"Fake?" Cindy asked, feeling a little light-headed.

"As fake as ninety-percent of this town is. There are four guards that work at that hotel and none of them look like the man you described. None of our officers on call last night reported anything like what you're talking about either, so I'm guessing even if I showed you pictures of every man on the force, you wouldn't find those two who took your thief away. The question is, what do you have that they want?"

"Nothing! I have nothing," Cindy said, her anxiety level increasing sharply.

"Maybe. Maybe not. It's also possible that they wanted you. Didn't you say they asked you to come with them last night?"

"Yes," Cindy said, growing still. That couldn't be the answer, could it? It wouldn't be the first time she was kidnapped. But to what end? She didn't have anything and she didn't know anything that could connect to the attack on Kyle.

"Is there anyone who would want to harm you?"

"No," Cindy said, taken aback by the question. "I'm just a church secretary."

And someone spent the last week trying to harm me so they could get at my friend who is former Mossad, she thought to herself. She hunched her shoulders slightly. What had happened last night couldn't have anything to do with that, could it? It was crazy to think like that, wasn't it?

Suddenly her black and white world seemed to be getting fuzzier around the edges. Maybe there were people out there who wanted to hurt her, and not because of anything that actually had to do with her. She was sure Jeremiah must have made enemies. Then what about Kyle? Was it possible that whoever had tried to kill him had gone after her because of him?

She pressed her fingers to her forehead, feeling a headache coming on. Things were just so complicated and confusing and they were getting more so by the moment.

"Are you okay?"

"I'm just...it's a lot to deal with, you know?" Cindy said.

Detective Sanders nodded. "I know it's a lot to process. It's not every day you find out someone might wish you harm."

Cindy barely managed to control a crazed laugh that threatened to escape her. Sometimes it seemed like the last couple of years her life had been filled with people who wished her harm. All those people should be dead or in prison, though.

She took a deep breath. "What do we do now?"

"I'm going to keep investigating. If you or any of your family can think of any detail that might be useful, please inform me immediately. Sometimes even the smallest, most trivial seeming thing can be the key to solving a case."

"Okay, what else do you want me to do?"

"Just be safe, and keep a lookout for anything or anyone suspicious."

"If you think this was deliberate, what are you doing to protect Kyle while he's in the hospital?" Cindy asked.

"We have a plain clothes officer keeping tabs at all times."

"Why plain clothes?"

"So that if we're right and whoever attacked him tries again they won't instantly spot the officer which gives us a shot at catching the scum. Also, if we're wrong, we haven't needlessly upset and worried everyone involved."

"What does the plain clothes officer look like?"

The detective shook her head. "It's best for everyone if you don't know that. I'm not even comfortable with the fact that you know there is an officer present."

Mark would have told her, but then again, they had a relationship of trust forged on too many shared bad experiences. This lady didn't know her from anyone. To her Cindy was just the sister of a potential victim.

"I'd also recommend that you stay with people, given what happened to you yesterday. Use the buddy system until we get this sorted out and figure out if what happened to you is connected to your brother or not."

"Okay," Cindy said. That was going to be a little bit difficult given the circumstances, but she would certainly be careful and on the lookout for any future attacks. "Do you still want me to give the descriptions of the men I saw to your sketch artist?"

"Yes, you never know what detail might be important."

Cindy spent the next hour trying to help the artist get the closest images he could of the fake security guard and cops. She'd never actually seen the face of the thief, and because of the hoodie he'd been wearing she wasn't even sure what hair color he had.

When at last they were finished she left the station with Detective Sanders' card in her wallet. She grabbed a taxi to take her to the hospital. The entire ride, though, she felt nervous and on edge and she kept looking around as though she would somehow see the black sedan that had hit her brother heading for her. It was a nerve-wracking ride, and when it was finally over she half-ran into the comparative safety of the hospital lobby.

Once inside she paused to gather herself. She didn't want to meet back up with her parents until she was at least marginally calmer. The last thing they needed was more stress than they were already dealing with. She didn't think they knew that the police thought that the accident had been an intentional attack. Part of her felt like they deserved the truth, but the other part of her didn't want them worrying more over something they couldn't control.

When she had finally gotten herself together she headed upstairs. Her parents were in the observation room, looking exactly like they had the day before. As she looked through the window she realized that Kyle looked exactly the same, too. It was like some weird case of déjà vu.

"Has there been any change?" she asked.

Her father shook his head.

She sat down in one of the chairs and found herself watching her parents just as much as she was watching her brother. She felt so helpless just sitting and watching. If they could have at least been in the same room as Kyle that would be different. She could hold his hand and talk to him even if he couldn't hear her or talk back. At least that would be better than this interminable silence.

Her mind was still whirling thinking about everything the detective had told her. She still had no idea what the thief and his accomplices wanted with her purse the night before. It was too elaborate to have been a random crime. She had to have been targeted.

Having the fake security guard and fake cops was the really odd part. It implied that the thief either expected to be caught or wanted to be caught. What was it they could possibly want with her to make that much effort worth it? Anyone who knew anything about her brother would know that they weren't close. Certainly not close enough for him to have given her anything important.

There was a flaw in their plan, though, if the thief had wanted to be caught. He would have gotten away if it hadn't been for Martin coming in the door at that exact instant.

Martin.

Was he in on it? His appearance at the exact right moment seemed like too much of a coincidence, especially given the fact that the thief had known he'd likely be caught. But if Martin was in on it, why go to such elaborate lengths? He'd been alone with her on multiple occasions. If he'd wanted to steal her purse or do something to her he'd had ample opportunity before that moment.

Sitting there in the silence with her thoughts tumbling together she felt like she was going crazy. She needed answers and there were none to be found in this tiny room. Even if she could get her mom to say more than two words she doubted the other woman was capable of thinking clearly enough to give her any useful information.

Lisa. She should talk to Lisa.

She forced herself to sit another fifteen minutes. After all, that's what it seemed like everyone expected her to do. Finally she stood up. "I'm going to go check in on Lisa and sit with her for a while," she said.

"Good idea," her dad answered.

She walked down the hall and entered Lisa's room. She stopped, staring around in surprise. "Did someone open a florist shop in your room?" she asked.

The room was absolutely filled with bouquets of flowers.

Lisa smiled wanly from the bed. "They all started showing up this morning. I don't know who most of them are from, though."

"It's impressive. Clearly you have some admirers and well-wishers."

Lisa shrugged. "My parents live here. I've spent time here. I guess that equals lots of flowers."

"Clearly it does. Do you want me to read you the cards?"

"Yes, that would be nice," Lisa said. "Thank you."

Cindy moved to the nearest arrangement, a massive spray of lavender flowers. "It says, 'Lisa, all our love and wishes for a speedy recovery Pat and Leslie.'"

"My cousins. They know that purple is my favorite color," Lisa said wistfully. "I was going to have the bridesmaids wear that color."

Cindy didn't like Lisa's use of the word 'was' because it implied that the wedding wasn't going to happen because

Kyle wouldn't pull through. She forced a cheerful smile on her face. "They *will* look lovely in this color," she said.

She moved to the next bouquet. It and the next two were from relatives. Cindy reached a bunch of sunflowers next which were already looking a little droopy. "Okay, 'Lisa, even the most lovely of flowers fade and die. Cherish every moment you have.' There's no name. And, that's kinda morbid," Cindy said turning to look at Lisa.

The woman's eyes were wide and if Cindy wasn't mistaken she saw fear in them.

"Hey, are you okay?"

Lisa nodded slowly. "It's...it's like you said, morbid."

"Any idea who sent these?"

"Not a clue," Lisa said, dropping her eyes.

She's lying.

Cindy stood, uncertain what to do. She felt in her gut that Lisa wasn't being truthful and that she knew who had sent the flowers.

"That's enough for now. Thank you for reading the cards," Lisa said.

"Um, sure," Cindy said, glancing at the remaining arrangements. She was suddenly very curious what other macabre sentiments might be written on some of the other cards. Lisa didn't want to hear any more, though, and she couldn't think of a way to keep reading them to herself without being rude and obvious that she was suspicious about something.

"Is Kyle...How's Kyle?"

"The same as yesterday," Cindy said, moving to sit next to the bed.

Lisa bit her lip and refused to look up.

"He's going to pull through, you'll see. You know Kyle, he's stubborn that way," Cindy said, trying to cheer her up.

"He is stubborn," Lisa admitted. "He asked me out four times before I said yes."

"Really? What made you finally say yes?"

"I hadn't wanted to date a celebrity. Kyle was cute, though, and funny, and romantic and the fact that he just wouldn't accept the no and leave me alone was actually quite charming."

"Nice to hear the word 'charming' as opposed to 'stalker'," Cindy said with a grin.

"No, he's too sweet for that," Lisa said with a sigh. "Before I knew it I had fallen for him. Hard."

"The feeling seems to be mutual."

Lisa touched her engagement ring. "Yeah, it does," she said softly.

Cindy cleared her throat. "Lisa, I know this is going to sound a bit odd, but is there anyone in town who doesn't like Kyle? I know he's filmed here before and he does have this amazing talent for annoying people."

Lisa looked up sharply. "You think someone would want to hurt Kyle?"

"I didn't say that," Cindy said, gingerly trying to backpedal. "I was just...thinking...you know."

Lisa shook her head. "No one that I can think of would want to hurt Kyle. He's a sweet guy. Arrogant sometimes, and totally obnoxious at times, but just a really good guy. He told me what happened on the cattle drive you were all on. You don't think another of his coworkers is crazy like that, do you?"

"I doubt it. I'm just a bit paranoid," Cindy said. "So, there's no one you can think of that has an issue with him?"

Lisa shook her head. "I mean, my mother wasn't as fond of him as I would like. She thinks I should marry someone more like my dad. She doesn't get that I'm different than she is. She'd never hurt him, though."

Cindy was now curious to meet Lisa's parents. The information about her mom not liking Kyle combined with her father's observation that they were strange made her very curious indeed.

"Cindy, if you don't mind, I'm really tired and I'd like to sleep for a while."

"Sure, no problem," Cindy said, standing up. "Just let me know if you need anything."

"Thank you," Lisa said, before turning her head away.

Cindy realized it was nearly lunchtime as she walked back into the room where her parents were. "Anyone hungry?" she asked.

Her dad stirred and looked at her. "Will be in a little bit. Would you mind doing me a favor?"

"Sure, what do you need?"

"We left your mother's pill case on the bathroom sink. Could you run back to the hotel and get it? I figure we'll be ready to eat in about an hour and she'll need it then."

"Not a problem. I'll go get it now," Cindy said, eager not to have to sit and wait in that room any longer.

She exited the hospital and was hyper aware of her surroundings as she crossed the street to the hotel. She didn't breathe a sigh of relief until she was safely in the room. She grabbed her mom's pill case which was right where her dad had said it would be.

She tucked it into her purse and wondered how much time she could take on her walk back. As much as she didn't want to sit in that room, though, she realized she wanted to be alone and vulnerable less.

Her phone started ringing. She checked it and saw that Jeremiah was calling. Her battery was nearly dead. She'd have to see if her parents had a charger. Otherwise she should be able to find one in the gift shop. She answered the phone. "Hi, could you call me on my room phone? My battery is going."

"Sure, what's the number?"

She walked over to the phone and gave him the number of the hotel. "I'm in Room 1412."

"Okay, bye."

The call ended. Seconds later her room phone rang. She answered and heard a series of odd clicking noises.

"Jeremiah?" she said.

"Get off the phone. Leave your cell in the room. Go find a payphone and call me," he said, his voice tense. Then he hung up.

Cindy slowly put down the receiver, wondering what on earth that was all about. She left her cell on the nightstand and left the room. Down in the lobby she stopped and asked one of the bell staff who pointed her in the direction of a pay phone. Fortunately it was in a glassed-in booth with a chair so she was able to sit and close the door which cut out most of the noise from the casino.

She put several coins in the phone and then dialed Jeremiah who answered on the first ring.

"Hello?" he said, voice still tense.

"Hey, it's me."

"Are you on a payphone?"

"Yes."

"Is there anyone nearby who can hear you?"

She looked through the glass doors of the phone booth. She could see people walking by, but they were all several feet away and none seemed intent on stopping.

"I don't think so," she said.

"Good."

"Jeremiah, what's going on?"

"I recognized the clicking sounds when you answered the phone in your room."

"I heard those sounds, what do they mean?"

"It means someone has bugged your phone."

Jeremiah grit his teeth in frustration. He should be there with Cindy, looking out for her, taking care of her. If someone had tapped her phone then they had big problems.

"You mean, someone is listening in on the phone upstairs?" she asked, sounding bewildered.

"That's exactly what I mean," he said.

"But why? Who?"

"I don't know. What's happened there since we talked last night?"

"Well, for starters, a thief grabbed my purse right after I got off the phone with you last night."

"What?" he asked, emotions roiling within him at the thought.

"It's okay. I got my purse back. Martin came into the lobby and I was able to shout to him for help. He tackled the guy."

"Who is Martin?"

"He's a salesman here at a convention. He was sitting next to me on the plane."

Alarm bells went off in Jeremiah's head. "And he just happens to be staying at your hotel?"

"Yes, it's the one across from the hospital. It's a medical convention and all the attendees are at this hotel."

While that seemed reasonable, he still didn't like it. It just felt too coincidental to him.

"But that's not the weirdest part," Cindy said.

"It gets worse?" he asked.

As she explained to him about her trip to the police station that morning he found himself tensing more and more.

"I don't like any of this," he said when she had finished.

"I'm not exactly loving it either."

"I should come out there."

He could hear her sigh on the other end of the line. "As much as I would like that, I'm still not ready to cope with having my parents and you in the same place. My dad was already under the impression from things Kyle had said that you and I are dating. I had to tell him that we're just friends."

Just friends. Suddenly he hated those two words with a passion. "Did he believe you?" he forced himself to ask.

"I'm not sure. If you came out here, though, it would certainly complicate things. Given the state my mom's in at the moment, I don't think that's a good idea."

"I'm not sure leaving you alone is a good idea, especially given what's happened already."

"I'm not alone. My folks are here."

"I should say it's not good to leave you unprotected."

"I'll be fine, and I'll call if anything else weird happens."

A year ago she would have been happy for him to go there and keep watch over her. She had grown, changed a lot since they first met. Was the independence she was displaying a sign of her own growth or a way of proving that she didn't need him anymore?

He was being crazy and he knew it. He heard the sound of her putting more change in the phone.

"That's the last of my coins," she said.

"I want you to check in with me twice a day, more if anything happens," he said.

"Okay."

"You can use the payphone, but go ahead and call collect."

"Okay. Should I do anything about the phone upstairs?"

"No, just avoid using it. Same goes for your cell. Only use it when necessary and never give sensitive information out over it."

"Oh, did you find out anything new about the Henry White case?"

"Yes, Lydia, the dead girl, was stalking him and I'm pretty sure that she was killed over something she took a picture of. We can't find a phone or a camera at the crime scene or in her car."

"Wow, okay, I've got to go. Bye."

"Bye."

He hung up feeling worse than he had at the start of the call. He didn't like the fact that someone had tapped her phone, especially when he had no way of knowing who or why.

You could find out who.

The thought came to him and he squeezed his phone tightly in his hand. It was true. There were calls he could make and he could probably even get some answers. Once he opened that door, though, there'd be no shutting it. He wasn't prepared for that. Neither was she.

Cindy sat in the phone booth for a moment, trying to digest what Jeremiah had just told her. Who on earth would want to bug her phone? She certainly didn't know anyone in the city and it wasn't like this was a planned trip and someone could have known where she would be in advance. The room wasn't even registered to her.

But it was registered to her parents. If someone had tried to hurt or kill Kyle it would explain their interest in his family. With Kyle under such close surveillance by doctors and family at the hospital it would probably be easier to eavesdrop than to get near him there. Maybe she was right and the theft of her purse hadn't been a random act. Maybe they were targeting her because she was Kyle's sister.

She still didn't know what someone would want with her purse, though. Unless there was something Kyle had that they wanted and they thought one of his family members might be in possession of it now that he was in the hospital. If that was true, though, why wouldn't the attackers have stopped even for thirty seconds at the scene and searched him while he was in the car? She should get the key to his hotel room at the Excalibur and see if it looked like anyone had ransacked his room searching for something. Maybe they would have assumed that he had left the item there and when they couldn't find it they had then figured he'd had it on him. She'd also ask her father about that.

The only other thing someone connected to the attack on Kyle could have wanted with her purse was to plant some sort of listening device like they had on the phone in the room. Jeremiah was clearly suspicious of that since he'd told her to not give out sensitive information over her cell.

Her head was beginning to ache. She had some aspirin in her purse. The thought of it reminded her that she needed to get back to her parents with her mother's medication. She stood up, clutched her purse tight to her body, and headed out.

She felt like she was being paranoid as she walked to the hospital, but reminded herself that it wasn't paranoia if people really were out to get her. She'd seen a bumper sticker that said something like that once. Maybe she'd have to track it down and hang it up in her house as a reminder.

She breathed a little easier when she entered the hospital. She quickly made her way to the elevators. She was nearly there when out of the corner of her eye she saw someone coming right at her.

She tensed every muscle. Her hands wrapped more tightly around her purse and she could feel the tension thrumming through her arm muscles. Her leg muscles coiled, readying to run. She forced herself to take a deep breath and then she spun to confront the person.

A couple feet from her a pretty blond haired woman came to a stop, clearly caught off guard by Cindy's quick movements. There was something vaguely familiar about her though Cindy was sure they had never met.

"Can I help you?" Cindy snapped.

"Um, I hope so," the other woman said, her brow furrowing in confusion. "You are Cindy, Kyle's sister, right?"

Cindy paused. The woman knew her name and she did look vaguely familiar, but she had no idea who she was. It was possible she was just one of Kyle's many fans. Given everything that was going on, though, Cindy was suspicious.

Before she could say anything the other woman nodded. "Yes, you have to be. I recognize you from the footage of the cattle drive trip."

Cindy blinked in surprise. "That show hasn't come out yet." She had always suspected, hoped actually, that it never would come out.

"Of course it hasn't. I saw some of it while Kyle and I were in the editing room at the studio going over shots for one of the new commercials the channel is going to air."

As Cindy realized that the woman must work with Kyle her face finally clicked. "You're Bunni, from that show Bunni's Best."

"Yes, Bunni Sinclair," the other woman said with a bright smile.

Cindy had caught a few snatches of the show on the Escape! Channel while flipping through. She relaxed slightly. "What are you doing here?"

"We heard about Kyle on the news," Bunni said, a shadow crossing her face. "We were shooting on location in Canada when we heard. A few of us piled in the car and we drove all night to get here. Everyone else is crashed out at a hotel, but I couldn't sleep without seeing him first."

"I understand."

"Yeah, unfortunately, they're not letting anyone near his room who isn't family," Bunni said with a scowl. Tears started to fill her eyes and she put a hand on Cindy's arm. "Is it as bad as they're saying?"

"I'm afraid so," Cindy said softly. It was clear that the other woman was truly worried and upset. She was an actress, but from what Cindy had seen of her show, she wasn't sure the woman was capable of faking emotion with this much realism.

"It's not fair. Kyle is such a good guy. I mean, he's got that wild and crazy reputation but under it all he's just really sweet and caring. Once when most of us were on location shooting a number of specials overseas, I got food poisoning. I've never been so sick in my life. Kyle stayed up with me, took care of me. He even drove me to the hospital and stayed until I was released."

"You must be really good friends," Cindy said, watching helplessly as the other woman began to break down.

"He was there for me, and I just wish I could be there for him."

"He needs everyone he can get in his corner pulling for him. At least his fiancée is doing alright."

"Fiancée?" Bunni gave her a stricken look. "He proposed to Lisa?"

Cindy bit her lip as she nodded. In a moment of insight Cindy realized that Bunni cared about her brother, really cared about him. She felt a great surge of pity for her. She was sure that Bunni was in love with him, and he was marrying someone else. That had to be a terrible position to be in.

A sudden image of Jeremiah marrying a nice Jewish girl filled her mind and she felt like she was going to be physically ill.

"Are you okay?" Bunni asked. "You're looking really pale all of a sudden."

"I'm fine," Cindy said, lying through her clenched teeth.

"Okay. Listen, can I give you my number? As soon as you have news, I'd like to know," Bunni said.

"You know what, I can do better than that," Cindy said, her heart really going out to the other woman. She reached out and took Bunni's arm, and pulled her with her over to the elevator. "Come with me."

"Are you sure?"

"Yes."

A minute later they were walking back into the observation room. "This is Bunni, she's one of Kyle's coworkers. She and some others drove all night from their shoot in Canada to be here," she said.

"He speaks very highly of you," her mother said.

Cindy blinked in surprise. That was the most communicative her mom had been. Her dad came forward and shook Bunni's hand. "He told us about one particularly exciting adventure you shared in an overseas hospital," he said with the ghost of a smile.

Cindy was pleased that Bunni had been telling the truth about that. She was even more pleased that her parents seemed to be accepting of her. She pulled the medication for her mother out of her purse and handed it to her dad. "Everyone ready for some food?" she asked.

"I'm not hungry," her mom intoned.

"You have to eat something," her dad urged.

She just shook her head.

"Okay, but I'm bringing you back a sandwich and you will eat it and take your medication then," he said.

"I'll stay here with her, if that's okay," Bunni said. She had already moved to stand next to Cindy's mom at the window and had one hand pressed to the glass and the other one pressed to her heart.

"That will be fine," her dad said. He turned to Cindy, "Let's go."

They made their way back down to the cafeteria. Cindy decided to gamble on the macaroni and cheese this time. They sat down at the table they'd had the night before and slowly began to eat.

"What were you up to this morning?" he asked.

Cindy shrugged, "I just had a couple of things to take care of."

"So you said. Everything okay?"

"Yes," she said, forcing a quick smile. She really didn't want to tell her parents about the purse snatching. There was no need for them to worry about it. At least, hopefully there wasn't.

Her dad looked at her oddly, but then dropped it. They ate for another couple minutes in silence. The macaroni and cheese was actually pretty good and she was pleased with her choice. Her mind, though, was on the things that she needed to do. One of them was check out Kyle and Lisa's rooms at their hotel. She didn't relish the idea of doing that alone, particularly if she had been targeted the day before. However, she didn't see that she had much of a choice in that.

"We were thinking of taking a trip out your way in the next year or so. See you, visit Disneyland and that theme park that's right near you."

"The Zone."

"Yeah, that one. Could be fun."

Cindy nodded. "Sure. There's lots to see and do."

"I know Kyle said that the Escape! Channel has been considering doing a series of shows in the area, particularly at The Zone. I think he said that Bunni's sister works there."

"Small world," Cindy said. "Where does she work?"

"He didn't say. Bunni seems really nice, though."

"Yes, she does."

The small talk was killing her, especially given all the things that were going on and what was at stake.

She took a sip of soda and put the glass down.

"Dad, do you know what happened to the things Kyle had on him when he was brought here?" she asked. "You know, like his wallet and stuff?"

Her dad nodded. "I'm pretty sure there's a bag of his stuff in the closet in the room he's in. That's how this sort of thing usually works."

"Ah, but we're not allowed in there to get it," Cindy noted.

"Why?" her dad asked with a frown.

She debated whether or not to tell him what she was thinking. She didn't want to worry him or her mom more than they already were, but if someone was really after Kyle they deserved to know the truth so they could be on the lookout for anything suspicious and protect themselves.

"I was going to see if I could get his and Lisa's room keys and drop by the Excalibur and grab a few things from their rooms."

"Does Lisa need some of her things?"

"I'm sure she probably does."

"So, she didn't ask you to?"

"No, but I thought I'd offer. If nothing else they might have some stuff, cameras or jewelry, that they'd rather not leave unattended in their hotel rooms."

It was a good idea now that she thought of it. No need to leave anything important lying around where someone might be tempted to steal it. Not that their room across the street was any safer. Still, she was sure they could work something out. Maybe she could give it to Lisa and she could keep anything of value in her hospital room or have her parents take it to their house.

He stared at her intently, and she focused in on her food. After a few seconds he said, "Care to tell me what you're really looking for?"

"What do you mean?" she asked.

"I don't buy the whole looking for valuables thing."

"What?" she asked, blinking at him.

"You mentioned a camera. You think they have one and that there's anything important on it?"

"I, I don't know," Cindy said, feeling flustered at being grilled. "It's Kyle, wherever he is there's usually a camera somewhere close by."

"You think that could be what this is all about?" her dad asked, leaning in close, eyes focused in on her like lasers.

"What do you mean?" she asked him.

Her father glanced around the room and then leaned closer. "I want to know if you want to search their rooms for the same reason I think someone needs to."

"And what would that reason be?"

"To figure this out," he said.

"I still don't know what you're talking about."

His eyes narrowed. "I'm pretty sure you do and that we're talking about the same thing."

"What is it you're thinking?"

"I think that whoever drove that car was trying to kill him."

Cindy stared flabbergasted at her father. "What makes you think that?"

"The same things I'm sure that make you think so, too."

"You're suspicious and paranoid?"

He actually laughed. "Yes, and I think you get that from me."

She blinked. "I do?"

"Honey, you know what I do for a living."

"You go into war-torn areas and help rebuild the infrastructure."

"Yes. It's not the safest job in the world. Sometimes people aren't overly thrilled to see me. Once, a long time ago, someone even took a shot at me."

Cindy gasped as fear bolted through her. She'd always been concerned about her dad when he was working overseas, but she had always believed that he was more or less safe.

"I never told your mother. It would have just upset her. I learned after that to be very vigilant, though," he said. "A few months back after that cattle drive filming debacle Kyle and I sat down and we had a talk. The whole thing scared him."

"It scared all of us," she said.

He shook his head. "I mean scared him like nothing has since he's been a grown man. He did a lot of hard thinking about his entire life, his priorities, his goals."

"And as part of that he proposed to Lisa."

"Yes. I think he decided that at the end of the day he wanted a little more stability and a little less excitement in his life. He also told me how you saved his life."

"I didn't do anything that anyone else wouldn't," she protested.

He smiled. "That's so like my little girl. You never see the things about yourself that are extraordinary."

"That's because I'm not. I'm just ordinary."

"You are far from it, but that's a discussion for another time. Back to the topic at hand. When I heard about the accident, it sounded to me like somebody deliberately hit Kyle and Lisa's car."

"I think the police are thinking the same thing."

He cocked his head to the side. "When did you talk to the police?"

It was time to come clean. "When I went down to the station this morning to give my statement concerning the guy who tried to snatch my purse last night."

"What?" he asked, clearly startled.

She grinned sheepishly. "Sorry, I didn't want to worry you."

"I think you should tell me everything from the beginning."

She quickly filled him in.

"I don't like any of this," he muttered when she was finished.

"Neither do I. That's why I want to get over to the other hotel and see if I can find anything in Kyle's room that might give us some kind of a clue as to who might have wanted to hurt him."

"We'll get the key as soon as we go back upstairs," he said.

"Great."

"You shouldn't go by yourself. I'll go with you."

"No, I don't think we should leave mom alone right now, regardless of what's actually going on."

He sighed heavily. "You're right. She's pretty fragile at the moment."

"Yeah, I mean Kyle has always been her favorite," she said. She stopped, horrified that she'd voiced that out loud to her father.

She looked at him, waiting for him to deny it. Instead he just looked at her with incredibly sad eyes. "She wasn't always like this you know," he said softly.

Cindy felt her heart start to beat faster. Was her dad actually admitting that her mom really did love Kyle more? Parents might have favorites, but they weren't supposed to actually admit it. That was unthinkable.

"What, what are you saying?" Cindy stammered, barely able to get the words out around the sudden tightness in her throat.

Her father reached across the table and took her hand in his. "Honey, we were all devastated when your sister...when what happened to her happened."

Cindy nodded, no longer able to speak.

"You were grieving, in shock. It was your first experience with death and having it be someone so close to you, and having it happen right in front of you...well, you were so traumatized that I don't think you really even noticed a lot of what was happening around you that first year. At least, not consciously."

He cleared his throat. "You and your sister actually look quite a lot alike. Every time we looked at you we were instantly reminded of Lisa and the fact that she was gone.

Your mother couldn't handle the constant reminder so she stopped looking at you."

Cindy felt sick inside as she scoured back over her memories of that year, fragmented and colored by grief as they were. She realized her father was right. Her mother had stopped making eye contact with her, would look over her head or at the floor when she had to talk to Cindy. She had never thought about it, although she probably had picked up on the avoidance subconsciously, especially since her mother had had no problem looking at Kyle.

"And you withdrew more and more into yourself, becoming more afraid of the world. Your mother did that, too, to an extent. She had always been a bit more adventurous, but she shut down that part of her life, too. Kyle, though, Kyle was out there tackling life with everything he had."

Cindy and Kyle had talked about that a few months before. While Lisa's death had driven Cindy to be obsessed with being safe, it had driven Kyle to take the risks and live the life he believed their more adventurous sibling would have had if she had survived.

"Your mom began to live vicariously through Kyle and all his adventures, basking in his triumphs, and, eventually, his fame. And all those years she was looking at him and not at you. When you make eye contact with people you feel more connected to them, more bonded and invested in them. So, yes, terrible as it is, your mother does love Kyle more. But I want you to know that it wasn't always that way, and it certainly isn't your fault."

A sob escaped Cindy. Ever since she had arrived the day before her mother had steadfastly refused to look at her, staring only at her brother. Looking at Cindy would only remind her of the death of one of her children and with another fighting for survival that reminder was probably the most painful thing in the world.

"She must hate Kyle's fiancée, because she has the same name as Lisa," Cindy burst out. She remembered her own negative feelings when Kyle had first told her his girlfriend's name.

Her father shook his head slowly. "I thought the same thing. In some weird way, though, she got excited, felt like she was regaining a daughter. Your mom's mind is a twisted place, and I'm sorry for what you have to put up with because of it," he said.

"You know what's weird?" Cindy asked, tears streaming down her face and onto her lips.

"What?"

"It's actually a relief to know, to understand. I wasn't wrong."

"And it wasn't anything to do with you as a person," he emphasized.

It actually felt like a weight was lifting slightly. She could never please her mother which meant there was no need to worry about trying anymore. She squeezed her father's hand, so deeply grateful for his honesty and his insight. "Thank you," she whispered.

"It sucks," he said, "but I hope it helps you to know."

She nodded, too choked up again to form words.

"We should have had this talk years ago," he said. She looked at him in the eyes with as much purpose as she could. Tears were shimmering there and he smiled at her.

"We're going to get through this," she told him.

It was his turn to just nod.

"I'm not that same little girl I once was," she said.

"I had noticed."

"And you know what makes me feel better when the world is crazy and painful and scary?"

He shook his head.

"Solving mysteries. Now that the mystery of the distant mother is solved, I think I want to figure out who did this to Kyle."

"I would like that. How can I help?"

Cindy wiped at her eyes with her free hand. "Help me get those room keys. I want to see if there's any clues to be found over at the Excalibur."

"Consider it done. You know, I've been amazed at the changes in you ever since you met the rabbi and started solving mysteries with him. I'm not sure if the credit should go to the mystery solving or to him. He seems to bring out a different side of you."

Cindy felt herself blushing. "We're just good friends," she said.

He raised an eyebrow and then smirked. "I think the lady doth protest too much. I wasn't implying you weren't anything but friends just now."

"Oh," she said, feeling herself blushing even harder.

His smirk turned into a full-fledged grin. "I see how it is."

"Dad, it's nothing," she protested.

"I believe you less every time you say that."

She glared at him. "You're impossible."

He chuckled. "I've been called worse in my time."

"How about we stop focusing on my life and start focusing on Kyle's and try to figure out how he got into this mess?" she suggested.

"Fine," he said with a sigh.

"Do you have any idea if anyone has a grudge against Kyle? It doesn't even have to be anyone here in Vegas."

"I've been wracking my brain, but I haven't come up with anything," he admitted. "Kyle really is a good guy and he doesn't by his nature make enemies. I was as shocked as he was with that whole thing last year."

"Well, when you are a celebrity I guess there are people who will always be jealous and want what you have," Cindy said.

"Just as long as it's not another coworker. I don't think he could handle that. It really rattled him."

Cindy thought about Bunni. "I have no idea if anyone he worked with was in town when the accident happened, but some of them are now. Bunni drove down with some others when they heard the news."

Her dad shook his head. "That poor girl. She has to put on a smile while doing some of the strangest things for her show. She does it, though. We watch that show sometimes, especially when it's on near one of Kyle's. She's got spunk, but it's like watching a train wreck sometimes. You know it's bad, you want to look away, but you just can't."

"I've only seen snatches," Cindy admitted. "I think once on Bunni's Best she was reviewing camping gear or something."

"That's one of the more interesting ones, take my word for it. Kyle has always liked her, though. Apparently she's a good friend."

Cindy knew that Bunni wanted to be more than just friends, but she kept that to herself. "Okay, so we can't confirm if there are any more jealous coworkers in the mix."

"No, so let's move on. There's the fans. Some of them can get a little obsessive."

"Do you think it could have anything to do with the fact that he had just gotten engaged?"

Her father frowned. "We didn't know about that until we got here. He kept it a surprise from everyone."

"Yeah, but he did propose in a hugely public way. It's possible that his fans or one of his fan's friend's saw it or heard about it."

"And what, decided that if they couldn't have him no one could? That seems hard to believe."

"I know, but like you said, some fans can get really obsessive. I mean one of my friends is a fan and even she got weird around him. She's not even one of the crazy ones."

"I don't think we're going to magically puzzle it out sitting here," he said with a sigh. "It probably is a good idea to go check out the hotel room. Maybe there's something there that can at least point us in the right direction. I do wish I could go with you, though."

Cindy took her last bite of macaroni and cheese and stood up. "Let's get this done," she said.

He nodded and after they dumped their trash they headed back upstairs. She was glad they had actually talked about it. It made her feel better and she was glad to know that her dad at least would be keeping a close eye on Kyle and her mom.

It took a couple of minutes, but Cindy was soon on her way to the Excalibur with both room keys in her possession. Lisa hadn't seemed at all suspicious about Cindy's request and had asked her to bring her a small jewelry case and her phone which she had left charging at the hotel when she and Kyle went to have dinner at her parents'.

Even though she was nervous as she got into the taxi, Cindy soon forgot her fears as she marveled at the Las Vegas strip. Massive resort casinos and towering billboards all blazed with lights. It was both beautiful and overwhelming. The road was packed with cars and the sidewalks were just as crammed with people walking. Up ahead she could see a white castle topped with red and blue spires. She couldn't help but smile. Her brother had always liked playing Robin Hood and King Arthur when they were kids. The fact that he had proposed in a castle, even if it was Las Vegas' interpretation of one made a lot of sense.

Past the castle she could see another resort hotel in the shape of a giant, gleaming, black pyramid. It was intriguing looking. She had never had any desire to come here on vacation. She wasn't a big gambler, but she was beginning to think you could just walk around and ogle all the crazy architecture and have a pretty good time. Billboards and signs on taxis advertised shows ranging from magic acts to Cirque de Soleil. She had never realized there were so many choices for entertainment in the city.

Who knew, maybe if Kyle pulled through this okay she'd come back one day and explore. If he didn't, then she knew she'd never again want to step foot in the city where her brother had been killed. She didn't like the dark turn of her thoughts and she took the opportunity to pray again for his recovery and safety and that they would find whoever was responsible.

The taxi driver finally pulled up in front of the Excalibur and after paying him Cindy walked inside. The sheer size of the place was breathtaking and she stood for a moment, trying to take it all in. Aside from the casino floor there was also apparently an entire shopping area and another area with stuffed animal carnival games for kids.

She finally made her way to the elevators that would take her upstairs to the rooms. Once she got off on her brother's floor she noticed instantly that it was quiet and the corridors were empty. Everyone was downstairs having a good time and it seemed like nearly a ghost town upstairs.

She found the two rooms she was looking for halfway down one of the halls. They were next to each other. She pulled out the keycard for her brother's room and took a deep breath as she wondered what she'd discover inside.

Cindy opened the door and walked in. She stopped short when she realized that everything Kyle owned was strewn across the bed and floor. For a moment she wondered if the place had been searched by someone. Then she relaxed as she noticed that all the drawers in the dresser were closed. In fact, it was just some of his clothes that seemed to be everywhere.

Kyle's room had always looked like this when they were growing up and he was having trouble deciding what to wear. As it turned out that was probably exactly what had happened since it was only dress clothes that were strewn about while shorts and T-shirts were still neatly packed in a suitcase.

She spent half an hour going over the entire room and she couldn't find anything that would shed light on the attack on her brother. Frustrated, she left the room and moments later she entered Lisa's.

She stopped in her tracks. In her brother's room there had just been some clothes strewn about. Here was different. Drawers had been yanked out of the dresser and dropped on the floor. The mattress had been slid completely off the box springs and was wedged between the bed frame and the wall. Everything Lisa owned was dumped in the middle of the box springs and her luggage was thrown haphazardly into the corner.

Cindy blinked in astonishment. Her brother's room had been messy. This one was in shambles. Lisa's room had been ransacked.

Mark had assisted one of the two police officers who had arrived in doing a thorough sweep of the dead man's room. While there had been nothing unusual in the bedroom, the bathroom had offered up one clue as to the possible cause of death. In the man's toiletries bag there was an epinephrine pen which suggested that the man had been afflicted with a potentially life-threatening allergy. It hadn't been used.

He thought about the dead man's puffy face and blotchy skin. He wasn't sure if there were poisons that could cause that reaction, but he knew that a severe allergy could. It seemed strange that if the man had enemies they would wait until he was out of the country to attack when it would be so much easier to kill him before he left or after he returned. A much simpler explanation might be that he had succumbed to a food or insect allergy of some sort and hadn't woken up from his nap to save himself with an injection.

Either way they had a lot more questions they needed to ask his widow. They finished searching his toiletries bag, but didn't come up with anything else of significance. Her toiletries bag was filled with creams, lotions, and a couple small glass vials of perfume. Most of the items had labels that proclaimed them to be anti-aging breakthroughs. He shook his head in bewilderment. The woman out there was in her early thirties and she looked fantastic. Besides, there was nothing wrong with a few wrinkles. They gave a person's face more character. What was wrong with her that she was so paranoid? He was very grateful that Traci wasn't that way.

They had just finished up in the bathroom as a doctor was arriving to take possession of the body. Mark shared their findings with the man before he and the local officer made their way to the manager's office.

The manager, the widow, the writer, and the other officer were all inside. Somehow it sounded like the start of a bad joke to him as he noted the occupants. With the way they were all positioned around the room, though, it felt like walking into some sort of Shakespearian tragedy halfway through the final act.

The widow was reclined on the couch with the manager kneeling next to her holding her hand. The writer, Elisa, was standing over the woman with her hand on the crown of her head. Across the room watching everyone was the officer.

When they entered Elisa looked up and caught his eyes. She glanced quickly down at the widow and then back up. He got the distinct impression she was trying to communicate something to him, but for the life of him he had no idea what that might be.

The thing that struck him most about the entire tableau, though, was the fact that the widow was stretched out on the sofa. In his experience most people suffering from grief or shock tended to curl their bodies up more, some all the way in the fetal position, but most just kind of hunched up, as if trying to protect their abdomens. Laying stretched out was more indicative of relaxation as it made the body more vulnerable. Sedation could produce that result as well, but he didn't think she'd been given anything. Her eyes looked too alert.

To him all that pointed to the fact that she wasn't nearly as grief stricken as she was letting on to be. It was possible she had not cared for her husband or that she was in some sort of severe denial about what had just happened.

"Nina, you're sure you don't know who was sending your husband the threatening letters?" Elisa asked.

The woman on the couch shook her head. "He wouldn't tell me."

"What did you find?" the policeman in the room asked Mark and the other officer.

"Not much," the officer standing next to Mark said.

"Did your husband have any severe allergies?" Mark asked.

"Yes, he was allergic to peanuts," Nina said. "How did you know?"

"We saw the epinephrine in his toiletry kit. It hadn't been used."

"Do, do you think his peanut allergy killed him?" she asked.

Mark shrugged. "The doctor will be able to say what killed him. The appearance of his face, though, is consistent with some kind of major allergic reaction."

"So, this could all be an accident instead of a murder," the one officer said.

"Something your restaurant served him killed him," Nina said, sitting up quickly and glaring at the manager who stared at her with a shocked expression.

"But, that is impossible, madam," he said.

"But it would be the simplest explanation," the officer said, his face registering a look of relief. If that was the case, it would certainly make the entire investigation easier on everyone.

"But, I tell you, that could not have happened," the manager protested.

"Liar!" Nina shrieked and lunged at him.

The man jumped backward, scrambling hastily to his feet. The officer next to Mark moved to restrain Nina.

"Everyone but the widow out!" the other policeman barked.

Mark didn't need to be told twice. He was out the door in a moment followed closely by the manager and then a few seconds later by Elisa who didn't look at all pleased at the turn of events.

Once they had moved a safe distance away the manager turned to Mark. "Please, you have to understand. It is quite impossible that we served him anything with peanuts in it."

"So many products have peanuts or peanut oil in them," Elisa said. "It's hard to guard against everything. Did he tell the servers that he had a peanut allergy?"

He shook his head. "He didn't have to. We all knew. He had contacted me months ago to discuss it in great detail. Our head chef went over every inch of that kitchen before he arrived to ensure that there was nothing that might harm him."

"That's a lot of effort to go through for one guest," Mark noted.

The manager raised his eyebrows at him. "We take the health and well-being of our guests very seriously here. We have a very exclusive clientele and we pride ourselves on ninety-five percent repeat customers. We are here to serve and to cater to every whim and need."

Mark had known Joseph had to have spent a lot of money on this vacation, but he was now starting to think that number might actually equal a small fortune. It was certainly the kind of vacation he and Traci would never be able to afford on their own which was just more motivation to get back to her and put this whole thing behind him.

"You'll want to tell the police about that so if it comes back as death brought on by his peanut allergy they'll know that this isn't just a simple matter of an accident caused by your resort."

"No matter how much Nina is going to want to blame you for it," Elisa piped up.

The manager nodded gravely. "This could not have been our fault and if the blame is put on the resort, it will ruin us."

"You said he talked to you months ago?" Mark said, remembering that Nina had said that the vacation had been a last-minute surprise.

"Yes. Like many of our clients he wanted to customize the experience."

"What does that mean?" Mark asked.

"It means that they'll be prepared to make some of your favorite meals, or provide you with the snacks and magazines you enjoy in your room, that kind of thing," Elisa explained.

"For your room, the gentleman who paid for the vacation requested the highest degree of privacy, new bamboo fiber sheets which provide superior comfort, and a few other things."

"Is that why those sheets are so amazingly soft? They're made out of bamboo?" Mark asked.

The manager nodded.

He'd never even heard of such a thing. He found himself wishing, though, that those sheets could make their way into his suitcase when it came time to go home. There's no way they would, but he could always dream.

"What kind of requests did Milt make?" Elisa asked.

"Aside from the food allergy requests, he asked for a lot of romantic touches, rose petals on the bed, that sort of thing."

"Anything unusual?" Mark asked.

"There was one thing. When he first contacted me he insisted that a large flower arrangement of lilies be waiting in the room when they arrived because his lady loved lilies. He called just a couple of days before arrival and told me that the lilies had to be changed to violets. He insisted and said it was very important. We, of course, accommodated him."

The manager glanced back toward his office. "If you'll excuse me, I want to make sure I get a chance to explain to the police about the steps we took to keep peanuts out of the kitchen."

He turned and hurried back.

"Well?" Elisa asked Mark.

"There's nothing left to do but wait," he said. "The doctor will report his findings and then it's up to the local police to figure out if there's anything more to be done."

She glanced around. There was no one in sight. "Could we talk privately?" she asked, her voice soft.

He nodded. "We're probably okay here."

She shook her head. "Come with me."

Reluctantly he followed. He didn't want to discuss Milt anymore. He just wanted to get back to Traci and the rest of his vacation. He was reasonably certain that Milt had died from his peanut allergy. Where or how he had gotten hold of peanuts he didn't know. Fortunately that was not his problem to solve.

A minute later they were in a small, grotto like area which had a bench swing. Elisa sat down on it and began to swing it back and forth gently. He stood in front of her, wondering what more she wanted.

"What are you thinking?" she asked without preamble.

"Excuse me?"

"About the murder."

"Well, for starters I'm not sure yet it is a murder," Mark said. "This could have easily been just an unfortunate accident."

"But you don't really believe that, do you?" Elisa asked, her eyes practically twinkling.

"I'm reserving judgment until I see the doctor's report. Or, rather, if I see the doctor's report. Hopefully my involvement in this mess is over now and I can return to enjoying my vacation."

"I'm just as eager to return to my vacation, but don't we have a duty to see justice done here?"

He stared at her in amazement. Unlike him this woman had likely paid for her own vacation here. That coupled with what Traci had told him about the writer meant she was probably quite wealthy. Why was she getting involved in something like this? Idle curiosity?

"Why do you care?" he asked bluntly. "It's not your job, your responsibility. You don't know them. In fact, it's really none of our business."

She looked taken aback. "Mankind is our business. The common welfare is our business."

He narrowed his eyes. "That sounds familiar. Are you quoting something?"

"Paraphrasing. It's from *A Christmas Carol*. It's what the ghost of Marley tells Scrooge."

"Ah, and I'm Scrooge in this scenario?"

"Well, you certainly are being miserly with your gifts and skills. You could help solve this murder for the good of all."

He sighed. "Fine. What do you want to discuss?"

"The widow, Nina, what do you make of her?" Elisa asked.

"Pretty, young, a bit on the dramatic side, but then again she has just lost her husband."

"I think she lost him before they ever came on this trip."

"What do you mean?"

"Given the differences in their age, I'd be willing to bet that she's his second wife."

"A trophy wife? I had figured pretty much the same."

"And they've been married six years. That's plenty of time for a man to lose interest and for a woman to start showing some signs of aging."

Mark couldn't help but think about all the skin care products meant to reverse aging he had found among her things. He shook his head. "That's crazy. She looks young and pretty."

"I'd be willing to bet back home there's some twenty-four-year-old who looks younger and prettier."

"You can't know that," Mark protested.

"Even if there isn't, she might think there is. After all, if he did dump his first wife for her..."

"This is just speculation. For all we know his last wife died or Nina could be his first wife and he married late. Unless you have something more substantial, I think we're jumping to conclusions."

"Did you see the bikini she was barely wearing?" Elisa asked.

"Yes, and yes, it was small, but what does that prove? A lot of women like to show off."

"Not many happily married women are willing to show that much skin. A bikini like that is meant as an attention getter which means she either wanted someone else's attention or was worried that she was losing her husband's."

Mark was ready to walk away. The woman's assumptions were so generalized and broad-sweeping as to be pretty much useless. "I suggest we let the local police handle this," he said. "That way we can both get back to our vacations."

He turned and started to go.

"You love your wife very much, don't you?" Elisa called after him.

He paused, not liking the personal turn of the conversation. "Of course, why do you ask?"

"Your own feelings of love and loyalty to your wife make it hard for you to acknowledge trouble in other people's relationships. Let me ask you this, though. When was the last time your wife wore something in public as provocative and revealing as that bikini?"

"Not since we were dating, but I don't see what that has to do with anything."

Elisa smiled at him. "And what would you say tonight if she showed up at dinner in a skimpy little dress that left pretty much nothing to the imagination?"

"I would ask her why she was wearing it."

"Exactly. Give what I've said some thought, Detective. I write romances which means I spend a lot of time thinking and analyzing how people in relationships interact with each other."

He nodded and then left. Even when she was out of his line of sight, though, her words were still echoing around in his head. By the time he found Traci on the beach he sat down beside her with a sigh.

"Honey, would you wear a skimpy bikini for me?" he asked.

Her eyes grew wide. "You know I don't like showing that much skin. Is there something wrong with the bikini I'm wearing? You're not worried about how fat I'm going to get while I'm pregnant, are you? Was someone else wearing a bikini and you were wondering how I'd look in it?"

He held up a hand to stop the onslaught. "Whoa, sorry, it was a hypothetical question based on a conversation I just had."

Traci took a deep breath. "Okay. Of course, if you really wanted me to, I'd wear it."

"Good to know. Seriously, though, what would make you spontaneously wear something like that?"

She didn't even hesitate before responding. "If I felt like you were ignoring me."

"And what if you thought I was looking at another woman?"

Her eyes narrowed to slits. "I'd kill you."

He couldn't stop himself from grinning. "That's my girl." He leaned forward and kissed her.

When he finally pulled away she was smiling serenely. "Remind me to threaten your life more often."

"It's a deal."

He just sat for a moment, staring into her beautiful eyes. He really was the luckiest man in the entire world.

She put her hand on his arm. "So, what was all that about?"

He sighed and turned so he could lay on his side on the beach blanket. "Elisa is convinced that the trophy wife was afraid that her husband was going to leave her for a younger woman."

"Trophy wife?" Traci asked.

"Oh, sorry. The dead guy's wife is like half his age."

"And I'm guessing she was wearing a really teeny, tiny bikini?"

"Pretty much."

"And we're sure she wasn't the one looking to find someone new?"

"We're not sure of anything at this point," Mark said. "Not even what killed him, although I'm pretty sure it was his peanut allergy."

"How tragic."

"I know. It makes you grateful for what you have...and, really, don't have. Tell you what, though, let's put all that behind us before I start wishing that Geanie and Joseph were here and we were the ones in Paris."

"Tahiti doesn't exactly go well with their Phantom of the Opera themed wedding," Traci said with a smile.

Mark leaned in toward her. "I don't know." He thought of the love song from the musical and he softly began to sing, twisting the lyrics slightly. "No more talk of murder, forget that dead man there."

"We're safe, nothing can harm us," Traci chimed in.

"Our embrace will warm and soothe us."

He folded her into his arms and kissed her, right there on the beach for all the world to see.

Cindy was standing in the hall just outside of Lisa's hotel room when Detective Sanders arrived. She looked harried and Cindy sympathized.

"So, you think someone has searched your future sister-in-law's hotel room?"

"Yes, I do," Cindy said.

"What makes you so sure?"

Cindy unlocked the door and shoved it open then stepped aside. Detective Sanders took one step inside and whistled. "Yup, that will about do it." She pulled a couple of pairs of disposable latex gloves out of her pocket and handed one set to Cindy.

"Did you touch anything?" she asked as she put on her gloves.

"Only the door. The moment I saw this I left the room and called you from my brother's room," Cindy said as she wriggled her fingers into the gloves.

"Smart. Then again, I'm not surprised."

"Why is that?"

"I did my homework. Turns out this isn't your first dance. Sounds like you've been at the center of some pretty nasty cases."

"Just unlucky that way, I guess," Cindy said, suddenly feeling self-conscious.

"Now, do you have any way of knowing what might be missing here, if anything?" Sanders asked as they stood looking around the room.

"Honestly, no. She just asked me to bring her jewelry and cell phone so those are the only things I would even know to look for."

"Well, the cell phone's over there," the other woman said, pointing to the floor near one of the bedside tables. She walked over and picked it up.

"Lisa said she left it charging, so whoever searched her room must have unplugged it," Cindy commented as she stepped closer.

"Oh, they did far more than that," the detective said, her voice grim.

"What?"

The detective turned the phone so that Cindy could see it. A picture of a skull with a sunflower between its teeth stared back at her.

"They left her a message."

"No way," Cindy blurted out as she stared at the picture of the skull with the sunflower.

"This means something to you?" Detective Sanders asked.

"Yes. Lisa got a bunch of flower arrangements delivered to her in the hospital. I was reading the cards to her. There was one arrangement, sunflowers, that had a really morbid message about death on it and no sender name. She was so upset by it she had me stop looking at the arrangements and reading their cards to her."

"Do you think she knows who sent them?"

"I don't know what to think," Cindy confessed.

"Is it possible they were targeting her instead of your brother?"

"I don't know anything. Maybe. Or maybe one of his crazy fans wants her dead."

"How well do you know her?"

"Not at all. We just met yesterday in the hospital for the first time. Kyle had told me a little bit about her a couple of months ago. I know she's an interior designer. That's about it really."

The other woman looked at her skeptically.

"I told you, my brother and I aren't as close as we could be," Cindy snapped, feeling tired and frustrated and somewhat embarrassed that she didn't know any more about his fiancée than that.

"Well, she and I are just going to have to have a little chat about all this. I'll call in a team to go over this place

WALK THROUGH THE VALLEY

and see what we might have missed. Unfortunately I can't spend more time doing it myself, but I only have so many hours in the day and Lisa isn't going to be questioning herself."

"Shouldn't you have a partner?"

"Should. Don't."

"Why?" Cindy asked, unable to contain her curiosity.

"Because I shot and killed my last one. Makes it surprisingly hard to get a new one."

Cindy started to smile, thinking it was a joke. Then she took a good look at the detective's face and realized she was completely serious.

"Sorry," Cindy muttered, unnerved by the revelation.

"Wasn't your fault."

She quickly changed the subject. She waved her hand to encompass the room. "What should I tell Lisa about all of this?"

"Nothing. I'll talk to her. Hopefully between the two of us we can clear some things up."

"What do you want me to do?"

"Nothing. You've already done too much. Go back to the hospital and be with your brother and your folks. I'm guessing you've already been in his room here at the hotel?"

"Yes, nothing out of the ordinary."

"Interesting. Like I said, head back to the hospital. I'll be in touch if I need to ask you anything."

Cindy felt completely deflated. Just when she felt like they were starting to get somewhere and she was actively doing something to help her brother the rug had been pulled out from under her. Given what Detective Sanders had told Cindy about her previous partner, she had no intention of pushing the woman for anything more.

"Bye," the detective said pointedly.

"Bye," Cindy murmured as she turned and left the room. A couple minutes later she was in another taxi headed back to the hospital. She had very little to show for her trip except for the knowledge that it was possible Lisa could have been the intended target and the fact that she knew pretty much nothing about her soon to be sister-in-law. Both things bugged her, refusing to let her mind rest.

When she finally made it back to the hospital she walked slowly into the observation room, miserable at the realization that there was nothing left she could do.

Her dad nodded at her, but didn't say anything. Cindy got the distinct impression that he didn't want to discuss her errand with her mom in the room. Cindy settled down in one of the chairs to wait. She lamented the fact that her phone was back in the hotel room where she had left it at Jeremiah's direction. It may be bugged, but she could at least have surfed the internet for a while, maybe done some research on Lisa. Without it, though, she was stuck in an information vacuum.

She glanced at her parents and suddenly realized that maybe she could obtain some more information.

"Dad," she said softly.

He turned away from the window where he was standing next to her mom and came to sit down next to Cindy.

"What is it?" he asked.

"I just realized that I know pretty much nothing about Lisa," Cindy admitted, wincing slightly in using that name in front of her parents. "You've spent some time with her, what can you tell me?"

"Well, she grew up here in Las Vegas. She went to school for design and has lived most of her adult life in different parts of California. She's nice, generous, thoughtful."

"She ever been married before?"

He shook his head. "Not that I've heard. I rather had the impression that she's focused mostly on her career since graduating from college. The dedication has paid off, too. Kyle says she's one of the most in demand designers in the nation."

"That's impressive," Cindy said, struggling with sudden, unexpected feelings of inadequacy. Her job wasn't that glamorous and she certainly hadn't had to work herself to the bone to make it to the top of her field. She forced herself to take a deep breath. Life wasn't a competition, not in that way. It was about being true to yourself. Besides, she had made a lot of valuable contributions to society in her own way.

"And what kind of work does she do?"

"All kinds. Everything from residential to corporate. She does a lot of high-end work. You know, one of the home design magazines ran an article on her this month. You might want to read it."

"Really? Which one?"

"I can't remember off the top of my head, but she's the cover story and it has her picture on the front. They might even have a copy in the gift shop here."

"You know, I think I'll go see if they do," Cindy said, eager for an excuse to escape the room of waiting. "Is there anything I can grab you?"

152

Her father shook his head.

Down in the hospital gift shop they had a number of books and magazines. As it turned out, the one she wanted was easy to spot because Lisa was indeed on the cover. She bought it and took it upstairs.

Once she had reclaimed her seat she opened the magazine and found the article. It was written by a woman named Majesty Starr and seemed to be a Q and A with Lisa. Curious, Cindy began to read.

Recently I sat down to chat up one of the hottest interior designers in the industry. Lisa Taggart got her start in her hometown of Las Vegas before moving to San Francisco and then finally on to Boston where she has designed for some of the most elite families in the country. She has since moved her business to Los Angeles where she caters to the rich and famous. Such A-listers as actor Jon Romeo have hired her to redo their homes.

M: Lisa, thank you so much for agreeing to do this interview!

L: No problem, Majesty. I love talking about design.

M: And the design community loves talking about you! To what do you credit your success?

L: Two things. First, I have a very strong sense of what I think looks good and doesn't and I bring that to every design project I work on. Second, I listen to the client, really listen. Sometimes they ask for things that you just know aren't going to work for a space. What's important is to listen for the underlying reasons behind their choices. Is there nostalgia at play or does a certain color make them feel a certain way or are they trying to replicate a look they've seen elsewhere? Once you understand what their larger, emotional goals are, you can help them create that even if you don't use the exact pieces or colors that they thought they wanted. At the end of the day the client has to be happy with the space and so do I because it stands as a representation of me and my work. If I give them something they want that's hideous other people are going to see that and they're going to blame me for the choice even if it wasn't mine. It might be my client's home, but it's my reputation which is why everyone needs to be happy with the outcome.

M: Wow, it sounds like you put a lot of psychology into your design work.

L: Yeah, I guess I do.

M: So, if I were to ask you to give me avocado green linoleum in my kitchen...

L: I'd find out what avocado green linoleum means to you and I'd find a different way to fulfill that need that still allowed your kitchen to be sleek and modern.

M: I guess that's the difference between a designer and a contractor. It's a contractor's job to give you exactly what you ask for.

L: And it's a designer's job to give you exactly what you really need.

M: Okay, forgetting for the moment about my avocado green linoleum question, what is the craziest thing a client has ever asked you for?

L: I've been asked for some really crazy things. I had one client who wanted a life-size marble statue of himself in the middle of the living room. Another one asked me for a glow-in-the-dark room where everything, including the carpet, glowed. One client had an obsession with sunflowers and wanted the entire house done with sunflower print carpet. Only one of these three clients got exactly what they asked for, but all of them were happy with the results.

M: Wow, I'm busy trying to picture all those things right now and they're all a bit overwhelming. Okay, getting myself back on track. Do you just do cosmetic work or do you actually restructure houses as well?

L: With the current obsession with open concept it seems like I'm always knocking down a wall somewhere or other. Honestly, clients ask me for a full range of services from just redoing the color palette of a single room to gutting an entire interior and rebuilding. Sometimes they want more rooms or extra space in the rooms they have. I've put in my share of panic rooms and safes as well.

M: Given your clientele list? I can imagine you have. So, do you think I should put a panic room in my house?

L: Unless you have something to hide or something others want badly I wouldn't recommend it. Mostly those are just a waste of good space, no matter how well designed they are. Spend the time and square footage on a nice master suite upgrade instead.

M: Good advice. Do you have a portfolio of work that potential clients can peruse either online or in an office?

L: No, most of my clients value their privacy so I don't make that kind of information available except in special circumstances. I do have pictures of all my work, but I don't usually show them.

M: They're more of a personal scrapbook then? Like your greatest hits?

L: Actually, they serve a far more practical purpose. I keep detailed files on each of my designs including sketches, swatches, and very detailed pictures. That way if a client comes to me needing something repaired, replaced, or replicated somewhere else I've got all the information I need right at my fingertips.

M: Have you ever had to use those files?

L: Absolutely. I used them for one client who was rebuilding after a fire. In that case they were a real life saver because the original furnishings were completely destroyed. Without my files we never could have recreated those rooms. I've had to dig up information on other client projects as well, but that was certainly one of the more memorable experiences. I was so glad I could help them rebuild and feel like they were getting their lives back.

M: I'm sure they were incredibly grateful. Unfortunately we are out of time, but I am very grateful for the time you've spent with me. Thank you for letting us all have a glimpse of Lisa's world where the sky is, I'm sure, a much better shade of blue than in most people's.

L: You're very welcome! It's always a pleasure to talk design.

The article concluded with contact information for Lisa's design office. It also included a humorous notation that if you had to ask how much her services were you likely couldn't afford them.

Overall, it was an interesting interview and Cindy herself couldn't stop wondering about the client who had wanted the all glow-in-the-dark room. She couldn't help but think about the church's youth pastor, Dave. He'd probably love a room like that and so would the kids. The other thing that had struck her was the part about the client obsessed with sunflowers. Could that have anything to do with the bouquet or the picture left on Lisa's phone?

Detective Sanders had instructed her to just sit and wait. Maybe, though, she could do a little more research and see if she could get Lisa to open up about the sunflower client.

Everything in her wanted to run to Lisa's room and question her as soon as possible. She forced herself to sit still, though, and take deep breaths. For all she knew the detective was in there talking to Lisa right now and wouldn't appreciate the intrusion. On the other hand, if the detective hadn't gone by to talk to Lisa yet Lisa wouldn't know about her room being ransacked and she would want to know why Cindy didn't have her phone and jewelry with her.

Cindy sat there warring with herself and her own indecision for a good half hour. She checked her watch and thought it might be time to call Jeremiah again and see how he was doing and give him the update from her end. She was getting hungry again, too.

Deep down she knew that even though she had a half dozen excellent reasons for leaving the room, they were all just excuses because she really, really didn't want to be there. She hated the silent waiting. It felt more like a death watch than anything else, and she refused to believe that her brother was going to die.

The revelations from her father about her mother's favoritism of Kyle just made things worse. The daughter that reminded her of the fact that she'd already lost one child was sitting in the room with her while she watched another child clinging to life. No wonder her mother wasn't even looking at her. She'd probably feel better if Cindy left. Her dad wouldn't, though, even if he had fallen back into a silent mood.

Patience had never been one of Cindy's virtues and now she felt every minute crawl by and it chafed her. Somewhere out there was the person who had done this to her brother, and they might go free. After seeing the sunflower on the phone and reading that article she was sure that Lisa must know something, or at least have her own suspicions. Surely she would want to get to the bottom of this as badly as Cindy did.

She had just about made up her mind to head over to Lisa's room when one of the nurses poked her head in.

"Miss Preston? Cindy?"

"Yes?" she asked, startled that the nurse was asking for her specifically and not one of her parents. Maybe Lisa had grown tired of waiting for her things and had sent the nurse to find Cindy.

"You have a visitor out at the nurse's station."

"Who is it?" she asked, getting to her feet. Maybe it was Detective Sanders. If so, she'd have to tell her about the article and what it had said about the client who loved sunflowers a little too much.

"He didn't give his name," the nurse said.

His name. It must be Martin. Maybe he was dropping by to see if she wanted to grab a meal.

"Thank you," Cindy said. "I'll be right there."

The nurse left. Her dad nodded at her and she walked out into the hallway. She left the ICU area. The main nurses' station for the floor wasn't that far from Lisa's room, so maybe she could at least look in and see if the detective was there talking to her. Hopefully she could do that without being seen.

As she walked toward the nurses' station she could see a man standing there with his back to her. He was wearing a tight black T-shirt stretched across broad shoulders. She looked around, wondering where Martin might have gone to. She didn't see anyone else, though, who wasn't a nurse. Could the man in the T-shirt be the one who wanted to speak to her? If so, who was he and what did he want?

She started walking faster, her curiosity trumping her caution. There were nurses bustling to and fro. Nothing could happen to her here without there being witnesses. Still, she tightened her clutch on her purse as she approached.

She glanced in the direction of Lisa's room, but couldn't see in. Cindy slowed as she approached the man, expecting him to turn at any moment. Her heart began beating faster. She finally came to a stop a few feet away from him.

"Is someone looking for me?" she asked, trying to keep her voice steady so as not to betray any of the anxiety she was feeling. The man cocked his head and then turned around.

She took a step backward in surprise as she realized that she recognized his face.

"Hank! What are you doing here?" Cindy asked, recognizing the assistant cameraman from the cattle drive they had taken with Kyle.

"I drove down with Bunni and a couple other coworkers when we heard what happened to Kyle," he said.

She stepped forward and hugged him and he folded her in powerful arms.

"Thank you," she said, overcome with a sudden rush of emotions at seeing a familiar, friendly face.

"It was the least we could do. Unfortunately, one of the other guys and I have to go. The boss needs us and it's an emergency. Wish I could say more, but I can't."

"That's okay. I understand."

"Bunni's staying though. I don't think you could blast her out of here right now," he said.

Cindy nodded.

"Anyway, I didn't want to go until I'd had a chance to say hello. I've got about an hour. Any chance I can talk you into an early, early dinner?"

"I'd like that," she said with a smile.

Every hour that he didn't know exactly where Cindy was or how she was made Jeremiah a little crazier. To try and relieve his building anxiety he had thrown himself fully into the search for Lydia's killer. After the police had not been able to turn up a camera or cell phone in Lydia's car, they had gone over every square inch of the church looking for one, but to no avail. It was clear to Jeremiah that whoever had killed her had taken it as well.

He kept thinking about what Lydia's roommate had told Liam about Lydia being upset Saturday and muttering that something wasn't right and someone needed to know something. If he was to go with the assumption held by both Cindy and Christopher that the politician was innocent, then it was a safe bet that he was the person Lydia thought needed to know something. It was possible she even had proof of it on her phone. That would track with someone killing her and taking her phone.

The questions that remained were, what did she know and who else knew she knew it? Jeremiah had gone back to her Facebook page where he had poured over more of the pictures she had posted. Unfortunately, her last update was Thursday morning, two days before her roommate last saw her. Whatever it was she had found out had happened sometime between then and Saturday morning.

He had checked Henry White's schedule, and the man had been at a rally Friday evening. Presumably Lydia had also been to that one. He was willing to bet whatever it was she had seen or captured had happened around that event. It was even possible that she had confronted her killer on Sunday with her information.

The only thing that made sense to him was that it had to be connected to the campaign or someone who was part of it. Otherwise why would she obsess over it? It was probably something she felt was hurtful or potentially hurtful to the man she idolized.

The more he thought about it the more he was convinced he was on the right track. He finally gave

Christopher a call and the man quickly arranged for Jeremiah to meet with Henry White himself in the late afternoon.

As he parked outside the hotel that Henry and his team were staying at he couldn't help but think about Cindy. She would have wanted to be here, to be part of this. He would have felt so much better if she was because then he'd be watching out for her every moment.

He checked his phone again to see if she had called, but there was nothing. Once he was done speaking with Henry he'd try to get hold of her if he hadn't heard anything from her yet. The fact that her phone was bugged was weighing heavily on him. He should be there with her, taking care of her.

He headed inside and Christopher met him in the lobby with an outstretched hand. "Thank you again for everything you're doing," he said. "Henry's upstairs with some of the key staff. We're putting our heads together trying to figure out what to do until he's proven innocent."

The team had taken over the top floor of the hotel, and Christopher led Jeremiah into a penthouse with some lovely views of the park he and Captain liked to go jogging in. There were half a dozen men in the room, all sitting in the living room area with papers spread out all over the coffee table.

"Everyone, this is Jeremiah who has agreed to help us," Christopher said by way of introduction. "Jeremiah, may I present Henry White," he said.

The politician stood quickly and shook his hand. "We're very grateful for the help," he said, staring earnestly into Jeremiah's eyes.

"Yes, we'll take all the help we can get," said the man sitting across from him. He also stood. "I'm Geoffrey Wells, the campaign manager."

Jeremiah shook his hand, noting that unlike his boss, Geoffrey did not meet his eyes.

A door at the far end of the room opened and Marjorie White entered. "What's going on?" she asked.

Geoffrey moved quickly over to her. "Jeremiah, the rabbi that has agreed to help clear Henry's name, has arrived. Come meet him," he said.

Jeremiah noted that Geoffrey put his hand on the small of Marjorie's back just above her waist and led her over. It was a rather intimate touch and he suddenly found himself wondering just how close the two of them were. He remembered that they had both already left the church on Sunday when the body had been discovered.

"Please, sit down," Henry said, waving Jeremiah to a chair.

As soon as he had sat down the politician leaned forward. "I'm so sorry about what happened to Lydia. I hope we can bring her killer to justice."

"The police are doing their best," Jeremiah said as he sized up everyone in the room.

"I've been told she attended a number of my rallies. I keep being haunted by the thought that if she hadn't come to the rally Sunday, she'd still be alive."

"We don't know that, sir," Christopher spoke up. "She might have had an enemy who would have killed her regardless of where she was or what she was doing."

"Maybe, I don't know," Henry said, looking doubtful.

Interesting. Henry was concerned that her death did somehow link to his campaign. Jeremiah wondered if there was some reason beyond the time and place of her death that made him think that. He would have liked to have spoken to the man for a few minutes alone without so many prying ears, but he got the distinct impression that even if Henry would go for that the others wouldn't.

There definitely was a strong feeling of anxiety in the room. Amazingly it was coming from everyone but Henry who instead was radiating sorrow.

"I want to help. I just don't know what to tell you, or even where to start to try to figure all this out. All I know for sure is, I didn't kill her," Henry said.

"I believe you," Jeremiah answered. "Unfortunately, I have no idea who might have wanted Lydia dead and that presents a problem."

It was true, but the odds were good it was probably someone in that room. These were the people with the most power to affect the campaign or hurt Henry. If only there was a way to flush out the culprit.

His phone rang. It was Liam.

"I'm sorry. If you'll excuse me, I have to take this call," Jeremiah said, standing.

"No problem," Henry responded.

Jeremiah stepped onto the balcony and closed the sliding door behind him. "Hello?"

"Just wanted to let you know that the only prints they found in Lydia's car were hers," Liam said, sounding frustrated.

"I'm here talking with Henry and some of his staff. I can fill you in later, but I'm pretty sure one of them is responsible."

"Oh, can you prove it?"

"Not yet."

A sudden idea occurred to him. "But I think I know a way to do it."

"How?"

"I'll tell you later. First, I've got to go back inside."

Jeremiah hung up and opened the sliding glass door and walked back into the room. "Well, I have some good news," he said.

"Yes?" Henry said, eyes hopeful.

"It turns out the police are going to be able to figure out in the morning who really killed Lydia."

"How, how are they going to be able to do that?" Marjorie asked.

"It turns out that the janitor had installed a hidden security camera that covers the wall of the church where the bathroom door is located. They were having some trouble with kids leaving graffiti and he set up the camera so they could catch the culprits. He's been on vacation and he'll be back tomorrow morning. He's got a padlock on his office where the monitors are and he's the only one with a key. The recording will show Lydia and whoever went into that bathroom with her."

He forced himself to smile broadly. "Don't worry. It looks like we'll have this entire thing cleared up tomorrow morning. Then it's back on the campaign trail for you, Mr. White."

"Please, call me Henry," the man said. "I sure hope you're right. I want to see that girl's killer brought to justice. I want to be able to look someone in the eye and ask them why they did that to her."

It was clear that the murder was haunting him. People reacted in different ways to witnessing violent crime or its aftermath. Clearly his experiences had deeply affected him.

If they didn't ultimately destroy him they would probably make him a better leader.

Jeremiah stood. "I should go. I'll call you tomorrow as soon as I hear anything."

"Thank you," Henry said, standing to shake his hand again.

Jeremiah nodded at the others in the room and let Christopher see him to the door. As soon as he made it to the car he'd have to call Liam and tell him the plan.

"You know, the next time you're going to set a trap, you might want to consult with people ahead of time," Liam said sarcastically.

"I had to improvise," Jeremiah said. "If it works you'll thank me because did you really need this case to be unresolved for another day?"

"Absolutely not," Liam said with a sigh.

"This way it's better for everyone, except, of course, the killer."

They were sitting huddled on the floor of the janitor's office at the church. The room was very dark with dim moonlight coming in from one window. There were no video cameras or recording equipment. Jeremiah had made all of that up hoping to lure out the real killer by making them think they had only a few hours to destroy evidence of their crime.

It was nearly midnight and they had been locked away in the office since before the church had closed up for the evening. Their cars were parked well down the street and not that far away other officers waited to close in on whoever showed up.

A few minutes later Jeremiah heard something. He turned and looked at Liam who nodded slightly. He'd heard it, too. Several seconds later there was the sound of metal against metal. Whoever was outside was using bolt cutters on the padlock, just like he had anticipated.

There was a clanging sound as the padlock fell off. Then the door swung open.

"Freeze, police!" Liam barked as he clicked on his intense high-powered flashlight. Caught in its beam Geoffrey struggled to cover his eyes.

Jeremiah heard the sound of running steps and moments later an officer was handcuffing Geoffrey. He had in his possession the bolt cutters, spray paint, a can of gasoline and some matches.

"Planning a little graffiti and arson to cover up your murder?" Liam asked.

"I didn't want to kill her, she made me!" Geoffrey babbled.

"Marjorie, your lover?" Jeremiah guessed.

"Yes," Geoffrey sputtered. "That girl had a picture of us kissing. She was going to tell Henry. It would have ruined all of us."

"No, not all of you, just you and Marjorie," Liam said.

"Marjorie said we had to stop her from talking, but she didn't want money! She wanted us to come clean with Henry."

"What did you do with her phone and the murder weapon?" Jeremiah asked.

"I threw them in the dumpster behind the hotel as soon as I got there. I - I didn't want to kill her," he broke down and began to sob.

"Take him to the station," Liam told two of the officers. He pointed to the two others present, "Go find that phone."

Liam took a deep breath and turned to Jeremiah after the others had left. "Thank you for your help, truly."

"You're welcome."

"Get some sleep. In the morning I'll need you to come in and make a statement," Liam said.

"Of course," Jeremiah said with a nod.

"Better make that late morning so that we both have a chance to get some sleep."

"Whatever you say."

"I'm off to go arrest Marjorie White for accessory to murder."

Jeremiah wanted to go home. He wanted to get some sleep. He thought about Henry White's face, though, and his promise to give him information when he had it.

"I'll go with you," he said.

Liam looked at him in surprise.

"Henry's been betrayed by the two people closest to him. He's going to need some triage counseling tonight."

"That's nice of you," Liam said.

"Don't mention it. Please."

They drove over separately, but went up to the top floor together. Liam knocked on the door and a minute later Henry opened it, eyes groggy.

"May we come in?" Liam asked.

Henry nodded and stepped back. He tied his robe tighter around his waist and closed the door behind them. He looked at Jeremiah and hope flared for a moment in his eyes.

"Did you find out what happened to her?" he asked.

"We did," Jeremiah said.

"Who is it?" Marjorie asked, entering the room. She, too, was wearing a bathrobe.

"It's the detective and Jeremiah," Henry said.

Marjorie stopped short and Jeremiah saw terror flash across her face. Liam stepped forward, handcuffs out.

"Marjorie White, I'm placing you under arrest for aiding in the murder of Lydia-"

The rest of his words were drowned out by her scream of rage.

"It was Geoffrey; he killed her. Not me!"

"We know. He also told us of your involvement," Liam said as he handcuffed her. He began to read Marjorie her rights as Henry turned bewildered eyes on Jeremiah.

"What's going on?"

Jeremiah put a hand on the other man's shoulder. "Geoffrey and your wife were having an affair," he said quietly. "Lydia took a picture of them kissing. She wanted them to come clean, tell you everything. They refused."

Henry stared at him, mouth gaping. At last he turned toward his wife. "That's why she died? You killed her because you were cheating on me and you were afraid I'd find out?"

"Henry, please, think about what it would have done to your campaign, your entire career. We couldn't let one little groupie ruin everything."

He held up a shaking hand. "She didn't ruin anything. That was all you, Marjorie."

Five minutes later Liam was walking Marjorie outside. Jeremiah watched from the balcony until he had put her in the back of his car and driven away. Then he turned to Henry who had sat down on the couch.

He went and sat in the chair near him and leaned forward. "I'm terribly sorry, Henry. I know this has to be hard for you."

"You can't even begin to imagine," Henry said, face ashen. "She really helped kill that poor girl?"

"Geoffrey said she was the one that pushed him to do it."

"You think you know somebody... It turns out, I didn't know her at all."

"People make mistakes. They do stupid things to cover up those mistakes just making the problem that much worse."

"Don't try to excuse what she did."

"I'm not," Jeremiah said. "I'm just saying that I'm sure the woman you married wasn't capable of doing this. Somewhere along the way, though, she changed."

"I don't believe people change. Not really, not their core personality. I appreciate what you're trying to do, but the truth is this really is all my fault. I chose a wife who was capable of murder. I chose her and then I gave her a taste of power. As soon as something threatened to take it away, she did as her nature dictated. Had I made better choices Lydia might still be alive."

"Maybe, but you can't know that for certain. All you can do is live such that her sacrifice means something."

Henry nodded. "You're right, of course, thank you."

Jeremiah nodded. The man was in pain and deep, deep shock. He was more lucid than many would have been, but he suspected that trying to reason his way through it and shoulder blame were part of Henry's coping mechanism.

Jeremiah called Christopher who came over. He was grief-stricken, but he struggled to keep himself together to try and take care of his boss. Jeremiah finally left as the dawn was breaking and drove home to get some sleep.

He slept very fitfully and rose a couple of hours later and headed straight for the police station.

"You look terrible," Liam noted.

"Thanks," Jeremiah grunted as he sat down at Liam's desk. "Let's get this over with so I can put this all behind me."

An hour later he was leaving the police station. In the parking lot he ran into Christopher.

"How's Henry doing?" he asked.

Christopher shook his head. "Not good, but a heck of a lot better than I would be if I were in his shoes. He's decided to continue his bid for governor, though, which I consider a victory. The state needs him."

"He seems like a good man," Jeremiah said.

"He is. And now he's taking this whole idea of walking through the valley even more personally. The state's in trouble and trouble is something he understands intimately, especially now. He's going to pour his own pain and anguish into his efforts to help save the state."

"That's not necessarily a bad thing."

"No. I think it will be the salvation of him. Maybe even of the state." Christopher shook his head. "I've got to go in and talk to the detective then I can go home and get some rest. When the story breaks later today we're going to all need to be on our game."

"Good luck," Jeremiah said.

"Thank you, really," Christopher answered as he shook Jeremiah's hand. "I owe you. The state owes you."

"Don't mention it," Jeremiah said.

"I'm sorry I'm not going to get a chance to say goodbye to Cindy, but we have to get back on the campaign trail." Christopher hesitated then continued. "About her, is she seeing someone?"

"Cindy is spoken for," Jeremiah growled.

Christopher took a quick step back and raised his hands. "Sorry, I didn't know," he said hastily.

"Now you do," Jeremiah said.

Cindy tossed and turned all night. It had been nice to catch up with Hank over their early dinner, but the man was as much of an enigma as he had been months earlier. At least she could finally put to rest her nagging doubts about Bunni, though. He had been with her filming when Kyle and Lisa were attacked. They had heard the news together and her shock and horror had been one of the driving forces that got them in the car and driving to Vegas.

After dinner Cindy had tried to visit Lisa only to find that the other woman was asleep. She had returned to keep watch with her parents before finally turning in for the night.

The next morning had consisted of more watching, waiting. When Cindy went to check on Lisa she found that her parents were there visiting. They were both incredibly well-dressed, but eyed Cindy with thinly veiled contempt that rattled her. She had no idea if the detective had been out to talk to Lisa. She was guessing she had, though, since Lisa didn't ask about her phone.

Cindy had retreated back to the observation room. Since noon a growing fear had begun to grip her. Something didn't feel right, and she couldn't put her finger on what it was.

She was just about to excuse herself to go call Jeremiah and find out how things were going with him when she saw activity in Kyle's room. The doctor was in there, clearly discussing something with one of the nurses. They were gesturing at a chart and then at some of the monitors that Kyle was hooked up to.

Cindy felt her stomach turn. Something in the man's posture scared her even though she didn't know why.

"Dad?"

He turned to look at her and she could see the fear in his eyes. Clearly she wasn't the only one concerned about what was going on. A second doctor entered the room and Cindy rose to stand at the glass next to her parents. More gesturing by the doctors. The first doctor shook his head.

"What do you think is going on?" Cindy croaked, barely able to get the words out around the sudden tightness in her throat.

The first doctor turned and left the room. Cindy turned to face the door and when he walked in the look on his face filled her with terror.

"I'm sorry," the doctor said quietly.

"What are you saying?" Cindy asked, clutching the back of the chair she had been sitting in earlier. In her peripheral vision she could see her father wrapping his arms around her mother.

"There's nothing more we can do for him."

She just stared at the doctor, struggling to understand what it was he was trying to tell her. His eyes filled with compassion as he stared at her. Finally he reached out and put a hand on her shoulder.

"You should go in and say your goodbyes."

16

Cindy ran into her brother's room, tears streaming down her face. Her mother's cries of anguish echoed in her ears as she fell to her knees next to Kyle's bed. She grabbed his hand. It was cold and limp and she pressed her forehead against it.

"Kyle, please, please wake up," she sobbed. "You've always been a stubborn idiot. Be stubborn now. Don't go. Don't leave us. Fight, Kyle! Don't give up. There are more crazy things you have yet to see and do. You're getting married. Fight for that. For her, if you won't fight for yourself."

She took a long, shuddering breath. Kyle remained completely still.

"God, please don't take him. Heal him right now. I know that You can, that You have the power. I'm begging You to heal him, to restore him fully. I believe that You can."

Her voice gave out as the tears started coming faster. She kept praying, though. She was dimly aware of her parents coming in. She could hear her mother sobbing. They were there for a while and then they left. A while later Lisa came in. She sat on the other side of the bed and cried and told Kyle goodbye.

Cindy wasn't going to say goodbye. She was going to pray and fight with everything she had.

Eventually Lisa left as well, and once again she was alone.

Cindy continued to kneel there on the cold floor. She lost feeling in her legs. The hand that was holding Kyle's eventually went numb as well. Darkness had fallen and the only light in the room came from the city lights outside the window. That was fine with Cindy. Her eyes were burning and more light would have hurt.

She heard a soft step behind her. A moment later a hand descended on her shoulder. Jeremiah. She didn't need to turn around to know it was him. Her soul knew his touch. She didn't know how he had come to be here, but she was grateful that he was.

Very softly he began praying in Hebrew above her. His presence and the sound of his prayers gave her strength and she continued on praying silently as he prayed aloud.

Hours passed and finally the sky outside the window began to lighten. A new day was dawning. Her back and her neck ached and she was weary to the bottom of her soul. Jeremiah was still standing behind her, his hand on her shoulder, praying.

Then Kyle's hand moved.

Cindy blinked, not sure she had seen what she'd seen. The hand that held his was numb. She stared hard and his hand moved again, there was no doubt of it.

"Kyle?" she said, voice quavering.

There was a groan from the bed.

Jeremiah ran outside and came back a moment later with a nurse.

Jeremiah tried to help her stand. Pain surged through her legs as the nerves came awake. Her legs started to buckle and Jeremiah caught her, lifting her up in his arms and stepping away from the bed as more hospital staff entered the room.

She lay in his arms, cradled against his chest and she looked up at him. "How did you get here? Only family was supposed to be here."

He smiled gently down at her. "I just told them I was your husband."

She smiled. "That's right. You're always my hospital husband."

"Always," he whispered.

He carried her into the observation room where she could watch through the windows as the doctor and nurses were busy examining Kyle. He was going to be okay, she could feel it just as surely as she could feel the strong, steady beating of Jeremiah's heart.

Every muscle in her body relaxed. "I'm so tired," she muttered.

"Go to sleep. I've got you," he said.

It sounded like the best idea she had ever heard. She felt him sit down in a chair, but he continued to hold her, cradled in his arms. She was glad, because she didn't want him to let go. Not ever.

Jeremiah sat with Cindy asleep in his arms as he held her. He breathed in the scent of her. The last couple of days had been torture. This was where he belonged, by her side, taking care of her, comforting her. All night he had stood and prayed with her, marveling at the depth of her faith and her courage. She was an extraordinary woman, one in a million.

Her phone was in the observation room on a table next to his chair. She must have left it in there the night before.

He picked it up. He'd check it over closely later, but there was something he needed to use it for first.

Her most recent call was from "Dad" and that was exactly what he was looking for. He called and held the phone up to his ear.

"Cindy?" a groggy male voice answered.

"No, just borrowing her phone for a second. I thought you should know that Kyle is waking up."

"What?"

"The doctors are in with him now, but he's regained consciousness."

"We'll be right there," the man said before ending the call.

Jeremiah put her phone back down.

Ten minutes later an older couple in rumpled clothes came barreling into the room. The woman went straight to the window where she could look in on Kyle. The man paused, staring intently at Jeremiah.

He moved toward him. "And just who might you be?" he asked.

"Jeremiah. I'm a friend of your daughter's," he said evenly. He shifted Cindy slightly so that he could extend his hand.

Her father shook it.

"I'm Don Preston, her father. Jeremiah, huh? I've heard a lot about you, mostly from Kyle. Nice of you to join us."

The man was sizing him up with shrewd eyes. Before Jeremiah could respond a nurse walked into the room. She looked at Cindy. "There's a couch in the next room. Do you want me to get your wife some blankets and a pillow?"

"She's not his-"

Jeremiah interrupted Don. "No, that's okay. I'll take my wife back to the hotel in a little bit."

"Okay," the nurse said before leaving.

"Something you should tell me?" her dad asked gruffly.

"They'd only let family back here," Jeremiah said. He was too tired to let it ruffle him.

"And you went for brother-in-law instead of just brother or cousin?"

"Cindy and I have seen our fair share of hospital visits and strict nurses."

"Aha, so it's not the first time you've told that fib."

Jeremiah let his silence speak for itself. He knew the other man was sizing him up. He had a shrewd gaze. Jeremiah knew the man had done contractor work rebuilding infrastructure overseas and had likely come into contact with a lot of interesting people he had to learn to size up in a moment.

Jeremiah just stared at him calmly, unflinchingly. Perhaps a little too much so. A normal guy would have been nervous and somewhat embarrassed under the circumstances.

Don looked like he was about to say something else, but he was interrupted by a doctor entering the room. The man looked bewildered.

"I don't know how it happened, but it looks like Kyle is out of the woods. He's going to be okay."

"It's a miracle," Jeremiah said softly.

The doctor nodded slowly. "It would seem so."

Cindy's parents hugged each other, tears of relief streaming down their faces. In his arms Cindy just slept on. He didn't wake her. She needed the rest, and besides, she had already known as he had that Kyle was going to pull through. It was great news, but whoever had tried to kill him in the first place was still out there and they were all going to need to be at the top of their game to stop him from trying again.

"You can go in and see him in a couple of minutes," the doctor said.

"Thank you," Don said.

He glanced over at Jeremiah. "She needs to sleep. Take her over to the hotel. Maybe get some rest yourself."

Jeremiah nodded. He would gladly carry her the whole way but that would draw too much attention to them both. He slowly nudged her awake.

When her eyes flickered open he smiled at her. "Kyle's going to be okay. You can see him a little later. Right now we need to get you back to the hotel so you can get some sleep."

She nodded.

"Are you okay to stand up?"

She hesitated then nodded again. Gently he set her on her feet. She swayed slightly, but he held onto her until she stabilized. He stood up and put his arm around her and she leaned against him.

They left the room and headed downstairs. After they exited the hospital they crossed the street and made it into the lobby of the hotel. They were just about to the elevators when Cindy pointed to a man about fifty feet away who appeared to be heading for the restaurant.

"That looks like Martin, I should introduce you."

"Later," Jeremiah said, staring intently at the man.

"He's probably going to have breakfast. I'm too tired to be hungry," Cindy commented.

They made it into the elevator and a couple minutes later they were in the room. She staggered over to the far bed, kicked off her shoes, then fell down.

"You should get some sleep, too," she muttered.

"I will in a little bit, I promise. I've just got something to take care of first," he said.

"Okay."

A minute later he could tell that she was completely out. Jeremiah quietly let himself out of the room, pocketing her key. He headed back downstairs and made his way to the restaurant.

"One for breakfast?" the hostess at the front asked.

He shook his head. "I'm joining a friend who's already here."

"Oh, okay," she said brightly as he walked past her.

Martin was easy to find. He was the only C.I.A. agent in the restaurant. The man was just taking a sip of coffee when Jeremiah slid into the chair across the table from him.

Martin slowly put the coffee mug down and looked him square in the eyes. "Good morning. I'm Rabbi Jeremiah Silverman."

"Nice to meet you. I'm Martin, traveling salesman."

"I know. I'm a friend of Cindy's. I figured it was time we had a little chat. I'd like to thank you for looking out for her as well as you have. You can relax now, though. I'm here and I'll make sure nothing happens to her," Jeremiah said, keeping his tone friendly.

"I'm glad to hear that. It can be a dangerous city, especially when you don't have a friend here."

"Yes, anything can happen in Vegas. At least, that's my understanding," Jeremiah said, allowing the corners of his mouth to turn up slightly.

Martin nodded. "It's unusual to see a...rabbi...this far from his home."

"Funny, I was just thinking how unusual it was to see a traveling salesman this close to his."

Martin shifted slightly in his chair. It was true. C.I.A. operatives weren't supposed to conduct investigations on United States soil. "You know, hard times, unusual times. That's what we're living in. Life is too short to just pretend everything is business as usual. Just last week I heard of a guy who died at a wedding out in California."

"Too bad for him," Jeremiah said. "He should have skipped the wedding and stayed home."

Martin was referencing the man Jeremiah had killed at Geanie and Joseph's wedding, the one who had been trying to hurt Cindy.

"Yeah, he was a party crasher, so I guess he got what was coming to him. Thing is, only people who will miss that guy are his brothers."

Jeremiah nodded.

"Of course," Martin continued, "a lot of people were wondering why he was there in the first place. Who knows, maybe he was chasing a ghost."

Martin was fishing. The C.I.A. didn't know who Jeremiah was although clearly they had their suspicions. They had decided to come at him sideways through Cindy hoping to find out more about him without having to engage him directly. Only their plan had backfired.

"Who can say why anyone does anything foolhardy?" Jeremiah said. "Wedding crashers, purse snatchers, people who stalk and spy on innocent young women."

It was a threat and Martin knew it. Jeremiah had just let him know that if the man and his team didn't back off of

Cindy, he was willing and able to do to them what he'd done to the man at the wedding. Threatening a C.I.A. agent wasn't necessarily a bright idea, but he was too tired to be subtle.

"Some people make promises they can't keep," Martin noted, an edge to his voice.

"I always keep my promises," Jeremiah reassured him. "When I was young I promised myself that someday I would be a rabbi. You know the thing about being a rabbi? I find it to be a very fulfilling career. I like it more than the job I had when I was younger. I like the lifestyle, the quiet, the communion with God and my fellow man."

And that was as close as he was going to get to actually telling Martin he was retired. The other man nodded slowly. "From what I can tell, you also like a certain church secretary. How's that working out for you? I imagine there are some real...culture clashes... there."

Jeremiah shrugged. "Issues of faith and bridging cultural gaps are the only things I'm interested in wrestling with these days."

"You sure about that?"

Jeremiah looked the man dead in the eyes. "I only fight the battles that I'm forced to."

"In that case, I hope no battles come looking for you."

"That makes two of us."

"Well, as it turns out, I'm probably going to be leaving the conference early. Pressing business elsewhere. I'm sure you understand."

Jeremiah nodded.

Martin leaned toward him slightly. "What will you tell Cindy?"

"The truth. It's better she hears it from me than from someone else one day."

"A bold move. I wish you luck with that." Martin reached into his coat and pulled out a card. He placed it face up on the table. There were no names or identifying marks on it, just a phone number.

Jeremiah glanced at it then back up at Martin. "I don't need to buy any medical equipment."

"Not now," Martin said with a smirk. "But keep it with you. Call me if you catch wind of any more wedding crashers. I'm sure my services might come in useful then."

Martin knew as well as he did that the dead man's "brothers" might indeed come looking for vengeance. Reluctantly Jeremiah reached out and took the card. He slid it into his shirt pocket.

"Good," Martin said. "I'm glad we understand each other. Give Cindy my best. I'll be leaving after breakfast and I won't get a chance to say goodbye."

"You traveling salesmen rarely do," Jeremiah noted as he stood.

Martin frowned suddenly. "Oh, Jeremiah?"

"Yes?" he asked, tensing.

"I'm not in the business of sharing gossip, but in my position, one hears things sometimes."

Jeremiah felt his entire body go still. He knew that whatever Martin was about to say was important.

"A handful of Israel's wayward sons are going to be called home. I don't know why. I just know it's happening."

"Thank you for the warning," Jeremiah said, forcing his voice to remain neutral.

"Whatever is going on between you and Cindy. You might want to sort it out sooner rather than later."

Martin was being sincere. Cindy had gotten to him. She did that. It was almost impossible not to like her, to feel protective toward her.

Jeremiah nodded. "Understood."

He turned and left the restaurant. His heart was racing in his chest and he could feel himself beginning to sweat. He had succeeded in warning off Martin, but the agent had given him something invaluable. Advance warning.

Retired Mossad agents were being reactivated.

Jeremiah made it to the room upstairs and his heart had finally slowed. In the elevator up he'd given serious consideration to trying to find out more information. He had a number he could call. By the time he'd reached the room, though, he had decided against it. His best hope was that he could remain under the radar. Hopefully whatever the reason agents were being reactivated it was something that could be handled by others. If he was lucky they wouldn't need him or his particular skills. The last thing he wanted to do was go back into the field. It would almost certainly cost him the life that he had spent the last few years building.

Cindy was asleep on the bed, sprawled on top of the comforter where he had left her. Her parents' bed was unmade with sheets and covers askew where they had risen quickly in response to his call about Kyle.

He had been up for almost thirty hours and he was tired. Don's suggestion that he get some sleep had been a good one. The only question was, how. The room was a mess indicative of the tremendous strain that the occupants had been under the last few days. There wasn't an unoccupied section of carpet big enough to stretch out on.

He walked around the bed Cindy was on and sat down on the far edge. He felt uncomfortable, guilty at the thought of just stretching out next to her and passing out. It seemed silly, though, in light of the circumstances. It was a big bed and they wouldn't have to be touching. Besides, they had slept next to each other in sleeping bags on Kyle's miserable cattle drive. He kicked off his shoes and laid down. Within seconds he was asleep.

As Cindy woke slowly she was aware that there was something different. She felt warm and comfortable. Her head was on something firmer than she remembered the pillow being. As she opened her eyes she realized that she had her head on Jeremiah's shoulder and one arm was flung over his chest. His arm was underneath her neck and wrapped around her back. He was breathing deeply and evenly with his eyes closed.

She lay very still, her mind kicking into overdrive. They had both been asleep in the hotel room. How had that happened? She barely remembered making it back to the hotel after finding out Kyle was going to be okay.

She didn't move. She told herself it was because she didn't want to wake him, but she knew it was more than that. It felt so incredibly good to be this close to him. She could feel her cheeks beginning to tingle with warmth. She stared at him, as though trying to memorize every line, every feature. It was funny because she realized she already knew them. As she continued to gaze at him she realized that she felt safe and contented and happy in a way she had never known before. She wished it could last forever.

His lips twitched and his eyelids flickered and she felt a surge of disappointment. This beautiful moment was coming to an end. What would he think if he knew she'd just been laying there watching him? She hastily closed her eyes.

A few seconds later she heard his voice and felt a rumbling in his chest. "Good morning."

She opened her eyes and found herself staring into his. Her breath caught in her throat and she felt her heart begin to beat faster. The moment felt charged to her. She should move, she should get up, but no matter how much she told herself to do either of those things it was like she was frozen, helpless as she gazed into his eyes.

"Did I ever tell you how beautiful you look in the morning?" he asked, smiling slowly.

"No," she whispered.

"I should have. You do. You always look so very lovely."

"Thank you."

He reached out with his free hand and brushed a strand of hair out of her face. Then he began to stroke her cheek with his fingers. Her skin tingled where he touched it. Slowly he moved his hand down to her throat and then her shoulder. He twisted his body so that he was lying on his side facing her and he wrapped both arms around her, holding her tight.

She felt herself flushing and her heart was racing faster and faster. She could feel his heart beating as well, strong and steady. He was staring at her, a smile on his face, and his eyes half-open as though he wasn't quite awake. His lips were only a few inches from hers and she could feel the warmth of his breath on her skin.

She was terrified, but there was a growing part of her that was feeling something else, something that threatened to take hold of her and not let go. She should say something, do something.

"I've never been this close to anyone," she said.

That hadn't been what she'd meant to say. Something funny would have been better, something to break this spell that was weaving around her head and heart.

He moved closer. His cheek brushed hers and fire raced through her. "Neither have I," he whispered in her ear, lips brushing the skin.

She shivered at the contact and he pulled back so that he could look at her again. His eyes were wide-open now, quickening with thought.

"What would my parents think if they saw us like this?" she burst out.

"Don't worry. I told them we were married."

"You what?" Cindy said, sitting bolt upright in shock at his words.

He remained where he was, but a grin spread across his face. "Okay, a nurse told them. Don't worry, I straightened it out."

She picked up her pillow and hit him with it. There were so many emotions coursing through her that she felt sick and dizzy. He quickly sat up, grabbed his own pillow and defended himself.

She squealed as he got in a good blow. She looked at him and he paused, staring at her in return, eyes questioning. "Game on," she declared and then swung her pillow at him with everything she had.

He jumped off the bed and twisted, taking the bulk of the force on his back. Then it was pandemonium as they raced around the tiny room, tripping over obstacles and narrowly avoiding knocking over the lamps. She was half-screaming, half-laughing and after a couple of minutes she was also gasping for breath.

Suddenly he caught her, pinning her hands and her pillow between their bodies. "Truce?" he asked, smiling down at her.

She struggled, but he was too strong and she couldn't break free.

"Truce," she wheezed.

He nodded and stepped back. She had the urge to hit him again with the pillow, but she had agreed to the truce, and if she broke that she knew all bets were off. She sat down on the edge of the bed, pillow still in hand. She hadn't felt this good in a long, long time. Kyle was going to be okay. Jeremiah was here and he was smiling and the pillow fight had been loads of fun and had helped her work through all the stuff she'd been dealing with the past few days.

Jeremiah's heart was racing and it had nothing to do with the pillow fight. In a flash he'd understood how much intimacy he assumed with Cindy. He took liberties with touching her that he shouldn't, that he had no right to. She wasn't his wife, no matter how many nurses he told otherwise. She was not his to hold in that way and had he been properly courting her from the beginning he would not have dared. But nothing about their relationship was proper or planned.

He thought about what Martin had told him. If Martin was right and there was a risk of being pulled back into his old life then that should simplify things for him. Somehow it didn't, though. It just made them feel more complicated. Martin was definitely right about one thing. He needed to sort everything out and soon.

He tossed his pillow onto the bed, literally and figuratively disarming himself. He sat down gingerly next to Cindy, close enough that they were almost touching but not quite. While he had been sleeping he had felt it when she rolled over onto his shoulder and he had not moved away. He had welcomed the contact with her.

"Cindy," he said, folding his hands in his lap and staring at them. "This thing between us, what is it?"

She had been fidgeting with her pillow, but she went very still at his question. "I don't know," she finally admitted, agitation in her voice.

He forced himself to look up at her. "Neither do I."

She licked her lips. "When I told you I'd never been that close to anyone, I meant that in more than just the physical sense. That was part of it, yes, but I've also never been this close...emotionally to someone else."

He wanted to reach out and take her hand so badly he ached inside. He forced himself to sit still, though. "Neither have I." He paused then continued, "There are a lot of obstacles in our way."

"A lot of differences," she said.

"We don't even share the same religion," he said.

"But we do love the same God," she pointed out.

"Your people believe they have found their Messiah."

"And yours are still waiting for Him to appear."

"You don't know everything about me, about my past," he said.

"Not yet," she countered. "But then, you don't know everything about mine."

"I'm not used to being lost, to not knowing my path," he admitted.

"I've felt lost for so long that sometimes I think if I ever found my way I'd be truly terrified."

"What happens now?" he asked.

She shook her head. "I don't know."

There was a sound just outside the door and a moment later it opened. Cindy's parents stepped inside. Don looked at Jeremiah. "Glad to see you're both awake."

Jeremiah wasn't sure if the interruption was a blessing or a curse.

"How's Kyle?" he asked.

"Better. Doctors say he should be fine. It's going to take several months for him to heal, but no permanent damage it looks like."

"That's wonderful!" Cindy said.

"They're actually transferring him out of the ICU."

Jeremiah stood quickly. "Who's watching over him?"

"The nurses I suppose. We came back to change into some fresh clothes and then we were going to grab some food before heading back over to see him once he's settled in the new room," Don said.

"Let's get over there," Cindy said, standing and heading for the door.

"What's wrong?" Don asked.

"If they're moving him he's going to be that much more vulnerable if his attacker wants to try again," Jeremiah said, following Cindy.

He heard her mom gasp, but he didn't have time to make sure they were okay. He and Cindy hadn't prayed so long and hard for Kyle just to have him killed anyway. He had no idea if Cindy had shared with them their suspicions that what had happened to Kyle wasn't an accident, but they could deal with all that later. They made it down the hall to the elevator and he tried to focus himself through the interminable ride down to the lobby.

They burst out of the elevator and ran across the lobby, then outside and across the street before making it back into the hospital. "We don't know what room," Cindy said, veering suddenly for the information desk.

"Kyle Preston's room number, please. I'm his sister and my parents said he was just moved from ICU," she blurted out at the startled woman behind the desk.

"Oh, okay, let me see. He's in...this computer is so slow..."

Jeremiah thought Cindy was actually going to leap across the desk and throttle the woman. For his part he was eyeing the group of people huddled in front of the elevator.

"Oh, here it is. He's in room 211."

"Stairs," Jeremiah said and ran with Cindy to the stairwell by the elevator. He yanked the door open and they went flying upward to burst moments later out into the hallway on the second floor. They raced past a startled nurse and burst into Kyle's room.

A woman gave a little yelp and scrambled to her feet from her seat on a chair next to Kyle's bed. "What's wrong?" she asked, hand pressed to her heart.

"Bunni? Is everything okay?" Cindy panted as she stared around the room.

"Yes, why? Is something going on?"

"How long have you been in here?" Jeremiah asked.

"I don't know, ten minutes or so. I came in right after they moved him in here," Bunni said.

Cindy dropped into an empty chair and struggled to regain her composure. She wondered if there was still a plain clothes officer keeping watch over Kyle like Detective Sanders had said there was the other day. She'd never actually managed to spot someone that she thought might be him. If there was one, why hadn't he responded to them running toward the room? Was it because he knew who they were?

"Hey, sis."

The voice was weak, but it was Kyle's. She got back up and walked around the bed to stand beside Bunni.

"Hey, how are you doing?" she asked, plastering a smile on her face and hoping he couldn't see how stressed she was.

"Okay. Been better, but hey."

"I was telling him about all the wacky stuff he missed out on while he was here and the rest of us were filming in Canada," Bunni said brightly.

Cindy nodded. "Bunni, this is Jeremiah. Jeremiah, Bunni is one of the other travel hosts at the Escape! Channel."

"Nice to meet you, Bunni," Jeremiah said.

She could tell he relaxed slightly knowing that Kyle wasn't in immediate danger.

"Yeah, she's the best," Kyle whispered.

"You're just saying that," Bunni told him, but her cheeks turned pink at the compliment.

A figure darkened the doorway and Cindy looked up to see her dad entering the room. "I convinced your mom to stay at the hotel. I figured it would be safer," he said, face grim.

"Everything seems to be okay so far," Cindy said.

Her dad moved farther into the room until he was standing on the other side of Kyle. "I'm glad to hear it," he said.

"We need to set up a watch so that two people are here at all times just to be on the safe side," Jeremiah said.

Cindy nodded. It was the smart move. A chill danced up her spine and as if compelled she turned her head and glanced outside. Two large men in suits were walking by in the hall. There was something ominous about them. One of them had his hand inside his jacket and the other was carrying a bouquet of large, yellow blooms.

Sunflowers.

They were heading toward Lisa's room.

18

"Sunflowers!" Cindy shouted as she bolted from the room.

She collided with a nurse just outside the door and fell, sprawling on the ground. She landed hard enough that the wind was knocked out of her and she lay there, clutching her chest in apparent agony.

Jeremiah swooped down to help her, but she shook her head and pointed down the hall. He ran, not sure which room was Lisa's so he looked in each as he ran by, scanning for someone with sunflowers.

At last he saw what he was looking for and he skidded to a halt and entered the room.

"Lisa, I presume?" he said to the terrified looking woman in the hospital bed.

She nodded mutely.

"I'm the rabbi. I've come to check on you to make sure your needs are being met. I know that they have kosher food options here at the hospital," he said, stalling for time.

There were two large men in the room and they looked like criminals in nice suits. Possibly some sort of mafia connection. One of them was carrying sunflowers and the other was pulling his hand out of his jacket, leaving the gun he had underneath it in place.

"I'm sorry it took me so long to come and check in on you, but I've had to make quite a few visitations, most of them to people a lot older and sicker than you," he said, forcing a smile.

He turned to the men. "Gentlemen, how do you do? I'm Rabbi Silverman."

They nodded at him, faces hostile. He pretended not to notice. In his mind he had already formulated a plan for how he would take them both down before they could draw their weapons. He was about to make a move when a nurse bustled in.

"Oh good, rabbi, I'm glad you found the right room," she said with a smile.

"Yes, thank you," Jeremiah said, realizing Cindy must have sent her. "I was just getting ready to have a nice chat with Lisa," he said.

"We should go," the first thug said to the second one. The second one nodded and put the bouquet of sunflowers on one of the tables. "See you around, Lisa," the first one said, his voice dripping menace.

Lisa didn't say a word.

The nurse bustled around, doing her duties. Cindy appeared a minute later in the doorway, pale but apparently alright.

Jeremiah walked over and stood next to her. "We scared them off."

She nodded. "I called Detective Sanders. As soon as the nurse leaves, though, I think we need to have a talk with Lisa."

"I think it's past time."

As soon as the nurse left Jeremiah pulled chairs up on either side of Lisa's bed.

"I'm, I'm not in the mood for company," she said.

"I'm not sure that's anyway to greet the man who just saved your life," Cindy said.

Jeremiah nodded. "Yes, because I'm pretty sure that's what just happened. Care to tell us who those guys were?"

"No," Lisa said, fear written all over her face.

"I know that whoever hit you and Kyle was coming after you, not him. That's what all the sunflowers are about. The ones with the morbid note, the picture someone put on your phone that I'm sure the detective showed you, and those guys with more sunflowers. Is this all connected to the client you mentioned in that magazine article who had the obsession with sunflowers?"

"Yes," Lisa whispered.

Cindy glanced at him. Now they were getting somewhere.

"Who is the client and why is he coming after you now?" Jeremiah asked.

"We can't help you if you won't tell us what's going on," Cindy said after waiting for several seconds in silence.

Lisa shuddered and it shook her entire body. Tears filled her eyes. Cindy reached out and took her hand. "It's going to be okay. We can help. We're good at this sort of thing," she said as reassuringly as she could.

Jeremiah nodded supportively.

"Shut the door," Lisa whispered.

Jeremiah got up and did so then came back to his seat.

"When I was just out of college, my parents wanted to help me out," Lisa said. "They helped me get my first design job with a...a friend of theirs. My father did some work for him."

"What kind of work?" Jeremiah asked softly, suspecting that it was not entirely above board.

"My parents own a restaurant. No one ever eats there, but a lot of money goes through it anyway."

"They laundered money for him," Jeremiah said quietly.

She nodded. "I didn't understand until I was an adult that that was what was going on. When I took the job redesigning his house, though, I already knew. I knew what he did for a living, but I needed experience. I needed work. So I said yes."

"What did you do for him?" Cindy asked.

"I redesigned everything. I mean, it was a dream come true, especially for someone just starting out. There were things, though, that he wanted that I knew...I knew they weren't right. But I did the job. I was afraid not to after a while. He had secret rooms put in all over for all kinds of things. There was a panic room and a few different safes. I designed an entire weapons room where he could store things. The more I gave him the more he let slip details about the things he needed and why he needed them. Then, the final part."

She came to a halt and tears started running down her cheeks. "He needed one last special room with a furnace that could burn at 1800 degrees Fahrenheit. I knew, *knew* what it was for, and yet I got it for him anyway."

That was how hot you needed it to burn to cremate bodies. He glanced at Cindy and could tell by the look on her face that she had come to that conclusion as well.

"I did my job. I did everything he asked. I even gave him his horrible sunflower carpet that he wanted. He said it was a constant reminder that life is fleeting and precious. I swore to myself that I would never again be in that position, afraid of my client. I finished the job and I left."

"But not before you took pictures of everything," Cindy said.

Lisa nodded. "I documented everything. I kept those files for insurance, you know, just in case. Then a few years passed and nothing happened and I thought...I thought I was safe. Then, when that car hit us, I knew it was because of him. In my mind I thought that it had finally caught up with me. I was just sorry that Kyle was there."

"He had read the article about you and suddenly he realized you probably had information about all his secret rooms, enough to give to the police if you ever wanted to," Cindy said.

She nodded.

"Where are the files now? Do you keep them at your office?"

Lisa shook her head. "No, not those. They are where they've been since the day I finished that job. They're in a safe deposit box here in town."

"Lisa, you have to go to the police with this," Cindy said.

"No! The only reason he hasn't killed me yet is because he doesn't know where they are, what I've done with them. He wants me to give them to him and that's what I'm going to do."

"Then he really won't have a reason not to kill you," Jeremiah said.

"He won't. He values my dad's services too much."

Jeremiah and Cindy exchanged glances. He could tell she was thinking the same thing. Lisa was a dead woman either way.

Mark had managed to go nearly a whole day without having to think about or talk about Milt's death. He could feel himself beginning to unwind. Vacation was definitely good for him and he couldn't tell how much of Traci's happy glow was inspired by Tahiti and how much was because of the baby. All he knew for sure was that she looked amazing and he couldn't be happier.

It was time for lunch and they had made their way to the restaurant. He was even getting used to the leisurely meals on the island. Lunch generally took two hours. Dinner took a minimum of three with course after course of food arriving.

As they entered the dining room he glanced around, noting the other hotel guests present. One table held a young family with a small girl who was asleep, her head resting on a stuffed bear. He continued to look around and winced slightly when he saw Elisa at one of the tables. Fortunately she was engrossed in reading something. The last thing he wanted to do was discuss Milt's death with her some more. He almost turned around and walked out, but Traci eagerly pulled him toward a table before he could.

No sooner had they sat down than Elisa made a beeline for them. She sat down opposite Mark and leaned across the table. "The police are here. Apparently Milt did die from ingesting a peanut product. They're with the manager and the head chef in the kitchen right now."

Mark groaned. That was almost certainly going to delay their own meal and he was starving. He turned and looked at Traci who was staring wide-eyed at the writer.

"Elisa, this is my wife, Traci. Traci, this is Elisa."

"Pleased to meet you," Elisa said, shaking Traci's hand.

"I love your books," Traci said.

"I think that might be an understatement," Mark said.

"It's always good to meet a fan," Elisa said with a smile.

Mark's stomach rumbled loudly.

"I'm starving, too," Traci said.

"Me three. I've been here for half an hour, but with all that's going on in the kitchen, I don't know how long before we'll see food," Elisa said, echoing Mark's own fears.

His stomach growled again.

"Okay, that does it. We have to get to the bottom of this so we can eat," he said, standing up.

He leaned down and kissed Traci. "I'll be back as soon as I can."

"Go get 'em," she said with a grin.

Mark moved toward the kitchen with Elisa beside him. "It's nice that your wife is so supportive," she said.

"She's beyond supportive."

In the kitchen they found Nina, the manager, one of the policemen from the other day, and the head chef. It looked like any other kitchen staff had vacated the premises for the duration of the inspection.

"As you can see, there is nothing here," the chef said, closing a refrigerator.

The manager and the policeman both nodded in Mark and Elisa's direction.

"It has to have come from here," Nina fumed. "My husband was killed by your negligence."

"Madam, I can assure you, we had nothing to do with it," the chef said.

"Nina, I thought you were convinced that he was murdered by one of his enemies from home?" Mark said.

She hesitated for a moment and Mark realized she was trying to decide which story to stick with. Confusion and fear warred briefly in her eyes and he knew in an instant that Elisa was right. Nina had killed her husband.

"Since he likely died within an hour of consuming the peanut product, the only people who could have killed your husband were the ones that had access to his food or drink at breakfast," Mark said.

She nodded slowly, clearly ready to jump on whatever theory he presented.

"If there are no peanut containing products in this kitchen, then we can rightly deduce that whoever had the peanut product added it to his food or drink knowing that he had the allergy and with the full intent of killing him."

"We have gone through the kitchen trash with the police. No one has disposed of anything there," the manager said.

"Which means that whoever did it took the evidence with them for disposal at some other place at some other time," Mark said.

"That would follow," the police officer said.

"And I'm guessing that person didn't realize that the kitchen had been so thoroughly prepped to be peanut free. They thought that surely there would be something, even a bit of peanut oil, that would be found and his death would be labeled an unfortunate accident."

He noticed that when he said the words "peanut oil" Nina turned noticeably paler.

"Are you saying one of his enemies followed him here and poisoned him?" she asked.

"No. I'm saying that one of his enemies arrived with him here and poisoned him," Mark said, staring meaningfully at her.

"Can you prove what you are saying?" the policeman asked.

"I think I just might be able to prove that Nina killed her husband, yes."

"That's a lie!" she shrieked, lunging toward him.

The manager grabbed her and pulled her back.

"How can you prove it?" the policeman asked.

"Have you allowed her to remove anything from the room where she was staying with Milt?"

"Not a thing. We sealed and locked the room."

"And we provided her with a few clothes and other such items from our store and moved her to a different room," the manager added.

"Then if I'm right, all the evidence we need should still be in her old room."

Nina began yelling and sputtering, growing more incoherent by the second. Mark only understood snatches of what she was saying such as "my property" and "sue the hotel". She was so out of control that he knew he had to be right.

Together they exited the back door of the kitchen and made their way to the hut where Milt had died. The policeman held on to Nina's arm the entire way. Once there, he passed the key to the manager who opened the padlock on the door.

They all made their way inside and spread out through the room. "In the bathroom you will find Nina's toiletries bag. There are a couple of small vials of perfume. I believe one of those actually contains peanut oil," Mark said.

The policeman handed Nina over to the manager who put a hand on her arm. The man then entered the bathroom and returned with the bag in question. He pulled out the first vial, sniffed it, then put it back. The second one was just over half empty and he opened the top of it and sniffed. He then placed his finger over the top and tilted a little of the liquid inside onto it. He sniffed it again and then touched it to the tip of his tongue.

"Peanut oil," he confirmed.

Nina visibly deflated.

"Why did she not throw this out?"

"She couldn't throw it in the trash in here because it would be noticeable. I'm guessing the reason she didn't dispose of it when she went to the beach and waited for him to die was just in case she needed to give him a second dose. He had an epinephrine pen in his things, but I'm guessing she was counting on him not being able to use it. Although, she might have tampered with it as well."

Mark walked into the bathroom and returned with the package in question. He nodded his head slowly. "Yes, look. It's expired by a few months. I'm guessing he wasn't the kind of man to risk his health given that he called months in advance to discuss the allergy with the manager. I'd be willing to bet she held on to this expired one and when the time came to get ready for the trip she swapped it out for a new one that he had, ensuring that even if he managed to use the pen it wouldn't save him."

"So, you've been planning to kill him for months?" the policeman asked.

"No! I just. I don't know why I kept that old one. I found the airline tickets to Tahiti last week. He was taking some other woman. I pretended that I hadn't seen the name on the second ticket. He wasn't willing to admit to the affair so he took me on the trip instead."

"That's why he called to change the flowers he wanted in the room so last minute," the manager said.

"I knew he was going to dump me, just like he did his ex-wife."

Elisa smiled at Mark. He nodded his head. She had called it.

"After all I did for that man! How could he?"

Nina dissolved into bitter sobs.

"On that note, I think our work here is done," Mark said. He turned to the manager. "Is the kitchen back open for business?"

The man nodded. "I'll tell the chef right away. Thank you for your help."

"You're welcome," he said.

He turned and left and Elisa went with him. As soon as they were out of earshot he said, "You were right about Nina."

"Good catch on the perfume vial with peanut oil," she said.

"Once I was totally on board with her being the killer, it all snapped into place. I'm just glad she wasn't a very good actress."

"Yeah, she wasn't very convincing in the part of grieving widow."

"No, and the fact that she kept vacillating between blaming mysterious enemies and the kitchen staff just raised alarms."

"She probably thought she was covering her bases. If she'd never brought up the whole idea that he had been murdered this would almost certainly have gone down as an unfortunate accident even when the police couldn't find any peanut products in the kitchen."

"Poor old Milt. He made a lot of bad choices."

"He married her for starters," Elisa said.

"And then he cheated on her. That was just asking for trouble," Mark added. "At least that's behind us now and we can enjoy the rest of our vacations. I didn't like the fact that work seemed to follow me here."

"I didn't mind so much. Solving mysteries has actually been a lifesaver for me," Elisa admitted.

"So, you do this often?" Mark asked, surprised.

She nodded. "I have a police officer friend in Hawaii. That's where I live most of the time. His name is Kapono."

Mark came to a halt. "You don't happen to know a police captain on Oahu, first name William?"

"Of course I do," she said with a cheery smile.

"Oh, you're the one," Mark said. When Jeremiah had been in Honolulu trying to find Cindy after she'd been kidnapped, his friend William had told him that he had his own version of Cindy, a female writer who was constantly finding dead bodies.

"I take it you've heard of me?"

"Yup."

He didn't bother enlightening her further. They had made it back to the dining room and Traci lit up when she saw them.

"Everything solved?"

"It was the wife," Elisa said.

"With the peanut oil," Mark added.

"Here in the dining room," Elisa concluded cheerfully.

Traci laughed and shook her head. "You two actually manage to make murder sound whimsical."

"One does try," Elisa said with a smile. "You must come by my room later, by the way. I have a copy of my new book which is coming out next month. I want to give it to you."

"For me?" Traci gasped in delight.

"Yes. Consider it a thank you for letting me borrow your husband for crime solving."

"Traci is the only reason I participated," Mark said. His stomach growled.

"Okay, that and I was hungry."

Cindy had gone briefly back to her brother's room to let her dad know everything was relatively okay after their abrupt departure. She finally returned to Lisa's room where Jeremiah was still trying to talk some sense into her. When she walked in and closed the door behind her Lisa turned red rimmed eyes to her.

"Please you have to help me. Kyle can never know about this," Lisa begged.

"This is the kind of thing you needed to come clean with Kyle about before the two of you became serious," Jeremiah said. He stared at Cindy. "He needs to know what he's getting himself into before he can make an informed choice."

"Kyle won't understand!"

"Maybe he will," Cindy said, staring back at Jeremiah. "Who knows, maybe he even suspected all along that there were things about your past that were dark, that you didn't want to share."

"Not Kyle. He's too sweet and naïve. He sees the good in everything and never the bad."

Jeremiah gave Cindy a slight smile and she smiled back. That was one thing she and her brother didn't have in common. She always saw the danger, the dark and scary things that could happen. It was Jeremiah who had helped her learn that just because you saw those things it didn't mean you could bury your head in the sand and hide from life. Life was to be embraced in all its terrifying, unpredictable glory.

"I just wanted to give people beautiful things," Lisa said, more tears beginning to fall.

"We understand, Lisa, but you have to understand that there are no more choices here, no moves to be made except one," Cindy said. "If you don't go to the police they'll kill you."

"Or, more likely at this point, they'll kill Kyle to send you a message," Jeremiah said.

Lisa began crying harder and Cindy felt a twisting knot in her stomach because she knew Jeremiah was right.

There was a knock on the door and a minute later Detective Sanders came in.

"What is she doing here?" Lisa asked, wiping her eyes.

"I called her while Jeremiah was dealing with the two thugs," Cindy said.

"I got here as fast as I could."

"I don't want to talk to her," Lisa said, sounding like a churlish child.

"We've gone way past what you do and don't want," Cindy said, hardening her voice. "That happened the moment you involved my brother. It's time to think of someone else's needs, someone else's future."

"She's right. If you care anything for that man in the other room, you'll do what's right," the detective said.

"But I'm afraid," Lisa whimpered.

"We're not," Jeremiah said in a strong voice. "We've been in worse situations. We'll help you find your way out of this one."

"I'd take them up on that offer. From what I hear about these two they're real miracle workers," the detective said. "And besides, if you run from this now you'll be running the rest of your life. And trust me that isn't a way to live."

Lisa took a long, shuddering breath. "What do I have to do?"

"You have to start by telling me the truth," the detective said.

"And then you'll have to tell Kyle," Cindy added.

Lisa nodded. "Okay."

Late that night Cindy and Jeremiah were sitting in a parked car behind one of the older casinos. Detective Sanders hadn't wanted them anywhere near what was about to happen, but Lisa had refused to go through with it without them there as emotional support. In the end the detective had consented, but Jeremiah and Cindy were parked a good two hundred yards from where all the excitement was scheduled to happen.

The detective was in another car with several police officers and Lisa was just arriving on the scene in a taxi that quickly sped away as soon as it had dropped her off. Underneath her arm she was clutching a file folder. After arranging for her to be released from the hospital earlier, the detective had instructed Lisa to pull the documents she had on the crime boss out of her safe deposit box.

Lisa had called the man to arrange a meeting whereby she would give him the documents and hopefully capture audio of him threatening her. Although the information in her folder was enough to allow the detective to obtain a search warrant, depending on what they found when they actually searched the man's house there might not be enough evidence to convict him of any crime.

Cindy was proud of Lisa for doing the right thing and agreeing to try and help put the man away. She just prayed that Lisa didn't get hurt in the process.

"I don't like this," she muttered to Jeremiah.

"Neither do I, but it's not our call. We're just here as spectators."

"Yeah, but I just can't shake this feeling that something's going to go wrong."

"All we can do at this point is pray for the best," he said.

She had prayed a dozen times at least already. Just sitting was going to drive her crazy, though. They'd been there for two hours already.

"Isn't taking down a mobster the kind of thing people get put into protective custody for?" she asked.

"Maybe. It probably depends on a lot of factors."

"Because if that happens, can you imagine? It would end Kyle's career. He might even have to have plastic surgery or something since his face is so easily recognizable."

"I think you're getting ahead of yourself," Jeremiah said softly.

She knew she was winding herself up, but she was scared for Lisa and scared for her brother. The next few minutes had the potential to change their lives forever.

"You're assuming that your brother is still going to want to be with Lisa when this is all over," Jeremiah said.

"Why wouldn't he want to?" she asked impatiently.

Jeremiah chuckled. "Not everyone is okay with their significant other having skeletons in the closet."

Cindy's nerves were jangling and she realized she should stop talking before she started talking about Jeremiah's past instead of Lisa's. Now was not the time. Not when she felt like she was going to jump right out of her skin and she thought for sure gunmen were hiding in every shadow.

She'd seen way too many movies about the mob. That much was clear. She took several deep breaths, trying to calm herself down, but it wasn't working.

Jeremiah reached over and grabbed her hand. He squeezed it hard. "It's going to be okay," he said softly.

She nodded and felt herself relax slightly. If Jeremiah said so a part of her believed it, no matter what nightmare images were racing through her brain.

Finally a car pulled into the parking lot and drove slowly toward Lisa. Cindy held her breath, hoping that whoever was driving wouldn't just run her down. After all, there was nothing to stop them from doing that. The car came to a stop, though, a few feet from her.

Several seconds passed and then a man with silver hair stepped out of the back seat. He walked forward until he was standing in front of the car. Cindy wished they were close enough to hear what was being said. She hoped that the microphone Lisa was wearing was functioning properly and that the detective would get everything she needed.

She saw the man gesture to the envelope. Lisa held it out. He stepped forward and took it.

And suddenly police officers burst forth from their hiding places and surrounded them, guns drawn. The man lifted his gloved hands into the air, the file clenched in one of them.

"It's almost over," Jeremiah said.

But Cindy knew from experience that was when things could go horribly wrong and the best laid plans fall apart. She kept scanning the area, looking for danger.

Suddenly she saw a figure step out of the shadows. He was holding something up. Whatever it was, it made Detective Sanders and the other officers lower their guns.

"No," Cindy said, reaching for her door handle.

"What is it?" Jeremiah asked.

"That's one of the fake cops who pretended to arrest the guy who snatched my purse," she said.

"Are you sure?" Jeremiah asked.

"Positive," she said as she got out of the car. She had to warn the detective and the others before something awful happened.

She sprinted forward. "Detective! Don't trust that man!" she shouted at the top of her lungs.

Detective Sanders turned to look at her and she tried to wave her back, but Cindy wasn't going to let the man get away.

The fake cop grabbed the mobster by the arm and pulled him back to the car. Why weren't the police stopping him?

The mobster climbed in the car and the fake cop started to get in after.

"No! You have to stop them!" Cindy shrieked, aiming straight for the car. She was almost there. Just another twenty feet or so.

She heard footsteps pounding behind her. Suddenly she felt something grab her around the waist and pull her backward. Her entire body jolted and she started to fall. Arms wrapped around her, picking her up from behind as she kicked and flailed.

"They're getting away!" she wailed.

The car reversed rapidly as the fake cop was closing his door. It turned and a moment later the driver hit the gas and with a squeal of tires it rocketed out of the parking lot.

Lisa collapsed to her knees, sobbing, while Detective Sanders and her men looked grimly on.

"Put me down!" Cindy shouted.

"Okay, but you have to calm down."

It was Jeremiah's voice. He was the one who had stopped her from reaching the car in time. Why on earth would he have done that? As soon as her feet touched ground she turned on him, furious.

"Why did you stop me?"

"Because I care about you too much to let you get killed," he said, looking deeply shaken.

His words penetrated the haze of rage and fear that had enveloped her brain. She teetered for a moment on her feet before regaining her balance. Then she spun to face the officers.

"That man!" she shouted, pointing in the direction the car had gone. "He was one of the fake police officers involved in my purse snatching. He was one of that guy's men. Why on earth did you let him get away?"

"It was out of our jurisdiction," Detective Sanders said, lips pressed tightly together.

Cindy stomped forward. "How is that even possible?"

The detective grabbed her arm and pulled her away from her officers and toward Jeremiah. She finally let go of her. "He was a federal agent, that's why."

"He was a fake cop a couple of days ago. He's faking being an agent, too," Cindy said.

Detective Sanders shook her head. "I don't think so. There's something bigger going on here. Don't worry, though, I intend to get to the bottom of it."

"How does that help her?" Cindy asked, pointing to Lisa.

"Well, he does have the file, and that's what he really wanted all along. I'm guessing he'll leave her alone now," the detective said.

"You guess? That's not good enough!"

It took half an hour for Cindy to calm down enough for them to get back in the car and head for their hotel. Between Jeremiah and the detective they were finally able to convince her that the man she had recognized was a real federal agent. What finally clinched it was a call from Detective Sander's boss asking her how she'd gotten into the middle of a federal investigation.

Exhausted and emotionally spent Cindy had her head back against the headrest in the car. "I'm sorry I snapped at you," she said.

"It's okay. It was completely understandable given the circumstances."

He had more he should tell her, but she was too exhausted and out of it at the moment. It could wait for the morning.

They made it back to the hotel, exhausted and ready to drop from the physical and emotional strain. They were about to head upstairs when Jeremiah's phone vibrated. He pulled it out and saw that he had been texted from an unknown number.

Restaurant. Now.

20

"Everything okay?" Cindy asked with a yawn.

"It's fine. I've just got to take care of something. I'll be up in a minute," Jeremiah said.

Cindy nodded and got on the elevator. As soon as the doors closed he turned and headed for the restaurant. He quickly discovered that Martin was sitting at the same table in the restaurant where he had met him before. Jeremiah warily took a seat.

"I thought you were leaving town."

"Unavoidable delay as it turns out. I'm sure you've encountered one or two of those before," Martin said.

"Slick way you intervened last night."

"A necessary evil, I'm afraid. We couldn't allow Mr. Russo to be arrested."

"So, he goes free."

"It's important that he does so. For now at any rate."

"You're running the man in some bigger game," Jeremiah realized.

"Give the man a prize. Truth is I was on my way to the city for a meeting with the man after a quick stop in California to investigate the circumstances surrounding the death of a certain terrorist who had popped up on the radar there. When I realized I was hitting a wall there I decided to catch the same flight out as Cindy. Two birds and all that."

"What's he doing for you?"

Martin shrugged. "Let's just say that Mr. Russo has few virtues. One of them is that he's a patriot. When he became involved in a business deal involving some very specialized weapons and some extremely unsavory characters he figured he had to do something about it. Being a savvy businessman, he made quite the deal for himself. He was afraid that the more we knew about him the more likely we were to cut him loose. Poor man didn't realize that the Feds had copies of everything in Lisa's folder ten minutes after she assembled it."

"And now?"

"Now we've made it clear to Mr. Russo that while we can be quite generous and forgiving business partners, if any harm comes to Ms. Taggart that will change. She should be safe. We'll find a way to let her know that so she doesn't have to spend her life running."

"Thank you."

Martin shrugged. "It's actually got nothing to do with you guys. She designed my boss's home theater a couple years back and his wife's been bugging him to have the kitchen and dining room redone next." He looked at his watch. "Gotta fly."

He stood and walked away. Jeremiah sat for another minute before getting up and heading upstairs.

In the room upstairs the curtains were open showing the Vegas nightscape. It let so much light in that he didn't need to let his eyes adjust very long. Cindy was already in bed, and, from the looks of it, asleep. He didn't blame her. It had been a long, stressful few days.

At the foot of her bed was a rollaway cot that her parents must have had delivered to the room. He was appreciative since it would cut down on the awkwardness of the situation. He took off his shoes, settled down, and he, too, was asleep in moments.

The next morning Cindy and Jeremiah ate a leisurely breakfast in the hotel's restaurant. She was worried for Lisa, but relieved that the nightmare was coming to an end. She was still struggling to piece it all together in her mind, though. They were sitting at a private table in the far corner of the restaurant with no one else around.

"You know, there's one thing I don't understand," Cindy said.

"What's that?"

"I'm assuming it was Russo who was behind that whole purse snatching incident. What did he want with my purse? Did he somehow think Lisa would have given me the documents?"

"Actually someone else was behind that," he said.

"Who? Was it the guys who took him?"

He was silent for so long that she finally looked up at him. She could see that he was struggling with what to say.

"I'm pretty sure this would be a good time for the truth, just in case you were wondering," she said with a hint of sarcasm.

He sighed. "Martin was behind that."

"Martin? What on earth for?"

"He's not a salesman. He works for the C.I.A. and he was investigating the man who I told you about, the one who was coming after you last week."

"The one you wouldn't just come out and tell me you had killed?"

He looked at her in surprise.

"Come on, it was kind of obvious from the way you phrased things."

"Yes, that man," Jeremiah said with a sigh. "He was an especially bad man with ties to terror groups and they were investigating what he was doing in the country and what happened to him."

"So he was spying on me?" she asked, feeling weird. It was like being told she had her own personal stalker. Her privacy had been violated and it made her anxious and vulnerable feeling.

"He was. Not anymore. He and I had a brief discussion, enough to satisfy his curiosity and get him to back off."

"That's just...creepy," she said.

Jeremiah shrugged and she realized that this kind of thing was part of his world, or, at least, was. They were going to have to have a much longer conversation about that, but it could wait until they were somewhere completely private.

They finished breakfast and headed over to visit Kyle at the hospital. In the lobby they ran into her parents who were headed over to his room at the Excalibur to pack up all of his stuff and check out for him.

"The doctors say he's going to be here a couple more days before he can be released. He's going to need a lot of physical therapy, but he'll recover. We're going to stick around and help him get home and set up," her father said.

Cindy nodded. "I'm just glad everything's going to be okay."

"Since he's out of the woods, you guys can head back home whenever you like," he said. "No need to take any more time off work than you already have."

"We'll make sure everything is cool here and head home tomorrow morning I'd imagine," Cindy said.

Jeremiah nodded.

"Okay." Her dad hesitated and then continued. "Lisa came by this morning and let us all know what had happened."

"Is Kyle okay?" Cindy asked, knowing that couldn't have been an easy conversation for any of them.

Her dad grimaced. "I don't think so. Well, we're off. We'll see you two a little later."

After they had gone Cindy turned to Jeremiah. "Maybe I should go alone and talk to Kyle for a few minutes before you come up."

"That's fine. I'll be down here in the lobby for about half an hour or so and then I'll come on up."

"Thank you for understanding," she said, spontaneously hugging him.

˙He wrapped his arms around her and held her tight for a minute. She closed her eyes and wished that the rest of the world would just fade away. When they finally broke free she steeled herself to go and face her brother.

A minute later she was walking into his room. Kyle had his head turned to the side and was staring out the window at the skyline.

"Good morning," she said cheerily.

"Hey," Kyle said, sounding tired and strained.

"You okay?" she asked as she pulled up a chair.

"The doctors say in a few months I'll be good as new."

"I heard, and that's great news, but that's not what I meant."

Kyle looked at her. "What do you do when you find out the person you love is not the person you thought they

222

were? That they have this whole past that's full of darkness?"

Cindy thought about Jeremiah. "I think that depends on you. How much do you love them and how much are you willing to just accept?"

"I've been dating her for a year-and-a-half. You'd think there would have been some sign, some clue. I feel like such an idiot."

"You opened your heart up to someone. That doesn't make you an idiot. It does make you blind sometimes, though."

"I guess."

Cindy took a deep breath. "I think the question is not about the last 18 months but about the next 18 minutes. Can you look her in the eyes and tell her that you forgive her, that her past doesn't matter to you and all that matters is your future together?"

"You're right," he said slowly. "You know the thing about nearly dying? It suddenly makes everything crystal clear. It strips away all the garbage, all the crap that isn't important and helps you really understand your life, your past, and what it is you want most. It's powerful. It's just sad that it takes something so awful to help you change your life."

"It's true, facing your own mortality does make things clearer," Cindy said. She knew that from experience. "So, can you forgive Lisa?"

Kyle's hands slowly curled into fists. "No, I can't."

Given his lead-up, that was not the answer she had been expecting. Obviously, though, it was one of the things that had been made clear to him. Cindy nodded slowly, her heart aching for him.

"Is that wrong?" he whispered.

"No," she said, reaching out to take his hand. "Everyone has different things they want, and different things they can accept when it comes to a spouse."

Kyle laughed a short, bitter laugh. "Want to hear something funny?"

"Sure."

"I just want a normal girl. A girl with no deep, dark secrets. Someone I can love who loves me."

His friend, Bunni Sinclair, popped instantly into her mind. She wasn't sure what she should say, though. "I think you're going to get exactly what you're looking for," she said.

"How can you be sure?"

"It's not my place to say," Cindy said, not wanting to interfere. Still, he needed some hope and it was clear that Bunni cared deeply for him. "I just think you might one day turn around and find that a girl you've known for a while, a friend, is the one you've been looking for all along."

"Thank you," he whispered.

She sat and talked with him for a little while, catching up on what they had each been doing for the last few months. Finally Jeremiah joined them.

After a while they finally left when the doctor and nurses needed to check him over some more.

"We'll be back later this afternoon," Cindy told him.

They made it downstairs and had just crossed the street when she heard someone call her name.

They turned and saw Detective Sanders walking up to them. "Glad I caught you," she said. "You folks heading out of town?"

"Tomorrow morning," Jeremiah said. "We wanted to make sure the dust had settled first."

"Smart. You should take in some sights, too. If you haven't walked the strip yet, you're missing out on some mindboggling architecture."

"What's going to happen now?" Cindy asked.

The detective shrugged. "It's out of my hands for now. The Feds have something they want him for, and I was told by my boss in no uncertain terms that I was to keep my hands off. However, that might not always be the case and I have a complete copy of everything Lisa had in that file. Maybe someday we'll bring him down. I'm just sorry all of you had to get caught up in this mess."

"We appreciate the update," Jeremiah said.

"Not a problem. Now that I've got that taken care of, I have to run. Things to do, bad guys to catch, and all that."

"I like her. She's an interesting person," Cindy said after the detective had walked away.

"I bet she has an interesting story," Jeremiah said. "I did like her one suggestion. I've never been to Vegas before."

"Neither have I. Want to see some interesting architecture?"

"I thought you'd never ask," he said with a grin.

They turned and headed for the main strip.

Several hours later they returned to the hospital. Cindy wasn't sure how many miles they had walked but she found it amazing how your mind played tricks on you when it came to judging distance here. She'd think something was only a few hundred feet away and would walk half a mile before she got there.

Jeremiah had explained to her that it was the desert that did that to you. Still, as tired as her feet were, she was glad they'd had a chance to just walk and ogle everything. They hadn't had any deep conversations, but there was time enough for that later. The last few hours had just been about unwinding and enjoying each other's company.

Upstairs in the hospital they ran into her father coming out of Kyle's room. "He's exhausted and falling asleep. I figured it was best to let him," he said.

"Where's mom?" Cindy asked.

"Bunni came by and took her out to dinner. I think girl talk was also on the agenda," he said.

"Dinner sounds good, I'm starving," she admitted.

"I know a cafeteria where the food is pretty mediocre," her father said with a smile.

"Lead the way."

"Oh, I forgot my phone in the room," he said, patting his pockets.

"I'll go grab it," Jeremiah offered. "I'll meet you guys down there in a minute."

"Thanks, I appreciate it," her dad said, taking her arm and leading her toward the elevator.

They made it downstairs and inside the cafeteria. Cindy moved toward the counter, but he stopped her with a hand on his arm. He pulled her over to the secluded table that they had shared that first miserable night. The look on his face was serious.

"What's wrong, Dad?" she asked.

"I needed to speak to you for a minute. Jeremiah. I know you care for him so don't bother denying it."

"Okay," she said cautiously.

"I just want to make sure you know what you're getting into."

"What do you mean?"

"He's a dangerous man, do you know that?"

"Yes, I know that," she said, trying to keep her voice as calm as possible.

"I've met one or two men like him in my day while working overseas."

"Dad, he's just a rabbi," Cindy protested, not wanting him to get overly concerned.

"Do me the courtesy of being honest with me right now. It's important."

She nodded.

"He might be a rabbi, but he wasn't always. I know how much you've always treasured safety, and there is nothing safe about that man. I would be a poor father if I didn't point that out to you."

"I know who he is." She hesitated and then continued. "And I know who he was."

"And you're okay with that?" he asked.

She looked her father straight in the eyes. "I am okay with it."

He searched her eyes for a long moment and then he reached out and hugged her. "That's all I needed to know," he said.

A couple minutes later Jeremiah entered the cafeteria. Her father grabbed her arm and pulled her toward the door. When they reached Jeremiah her father clapped him on the back.

"Change of plans. I've had enough of hospital food. What say we go to one of the steakhouses in town and get a real meal? I'm buying."

Jeremiah smiled. "Sounds good to me."

"Me, too," Cindy said, realizing that she couldn't stop grinning. Kyle might not be able to overlook Lisa's past, but Cindy embraced Jeremiah's. It was what made him the man he was today. The man she had fallen in love with.

Look for

THE SHADOW OF DEATH

The next book in the Psalm 23 Mysteries series

Coming July 2014

Look for

FEAR NO EVIL

Book #10 in the Psalm 23 Mysteries series

Coming October 2014

Debbie Viguié is the New York Times Bestselling author of more than two dozen novels including the *Wicked* series, the *Crusade* series and the *Wolf Springs Chronicles* series co-authored with Nancy Holder. Debbie also writes thrillers including *The Psalm 23 Mysteries,* the *Kiss* trilogy, and the *Witch Hunt* trilogy. When Debbie isn't busy writing she enjoys spending time with her husband, Scott, visiting theme parks. They live in Florida with their cat, Schrödinger.

Made in the USA
San Bernardino, CA
22 June 2014